Fragile
Dreams

Other books in this series for teenagers:

The Broken Stone
Dance to the Music

Other books by the same author:

Auntie Maude's Windmill
The Firebrand
God's Gloves
One Day in the Park

Fragile Dreams

Jennifer Rees Larcombe

Marshall Pickering

Pickering and Inglis
Marshall Pickering
3 Beggarwood Lane, Basingstoke, Hants RG23 7LP, UK.

Copyright © 1988 Jennifer Rees-Larcombe

First published in 1988 by Pickering and Inglis Ltd
Part of the Marshall Pickering Holdings Group
A subsidary of the Zondervan Corporation

ISBN 0-7208-0714-X

Text Set in 10/12pt Plantin by Brian Robinson Ltd. Buckingham.

Printed in Great Britain by Richard Clay plc, Bungay, Suffolk.

*To my daughter Naomi
who made me rewrite this
book many many times!*

Preface

This book is the third in the series. *The Broken Stone* and *Dance to the Music* come first, but *Fragile Dreams* is complete in itself, so it won't matter if you read the books in the wrong order.

Here is a brief introduction to the main characters.

Manda. She was disgusted when her mother decided to foster a girl of 15, the same age as herself, yet her rage gave way to an uneasy fear when she first met Mary Jenkins. Soon this strange and gifted girl hypnotised her into becoming her unwilling slave and constant shadow.

Sheesha. She was abandoned in London at the age of two with an evil amulet round her neck and a strange letter in the pocket of her little jacket.

She was renamed Mary and adopted by Mrs Jenkins who soon found she had taken on more than she could manage. Little Mary was gifted to the point of genius. When Mrs Jenkins become ill she thankfully had Mary taken into care by the local authority and she was placed finally with Manda's family.

When Mrs Jenkins died the strange letter was found among her possessions and given to Mary. It was written by her mother, an Indian girl who had been lured away from her home and country by a cruel Englishman who had abandoned her and her baby daughter in London

Her health had broken and she intended to kill herself and the letter finished with the words, 'Avenge my death.'

'I will!' swore Mary as she read the letter. 'I will find my real father, and when I do I will kill him.'

Finding him proved difficult even for someone with such a high intelligence, so Mary turned to the black arts of witchcraft and became involved with a phoney medium in London. She said she could trace her father through seances but she would need a lot of money.

So Mary began a blackmail and protection racket in her school, Gravely Comprehensive, and even turned to pushing drugs to raise money. When she was found out and was expelled, Manda's parents turned her out and she was sent to Parkfield Place, a residential centre for delinquent girls. The night before she left, however, she had one last desperate attempt to find her father with the help of her ouija board. But instead of telling her what she wanted to know it spelt out the terrible message 'On St Valentine's Day, Mary Jenkins will be no more.' She had only ten more days to live . . .

Doctor Davidson. He was Manda's family GP and the first time he met Mary he felt an odd bond between them. Twenty years before he had made a disastrous marriage. His wife was heavily into the occult and practised black magic. The day their baby daughter Meggan was born she said to her husband, 'I will make her a witch too Michael'. But she was far too deeply involved with her evil 'work' to care for her baby, leaving her to cry in her pram for hours. As soon as little Meggan could walk she followed her father around all the time, and this infuriated her mother. When she decided to fly to India to join the secret society she was involved with she took Meggan with her, but not wishing to be hampered by the two-year-old child, she abandoned her in London before she got onto the plane, which later crashed into the sea. Not however before she had hung her evil amulet round the child's neck and concocted a lying letter to plant hatred in the mind of her daughter in future years.

Poor Michael thought he had lost his little Meggan in the crash and he never quite got over the grief. When he met Mary he realised she would be about the same age as his Meggan and he longed to do something to help this lonely isolated girl.

When he became engaged to Manda's Aunt Beth, they secretly decided to adopt Mary when they could get her out of Parkfield. On St Valentine's Day Manda realised that Mary, or Sheesha as she always called her, would be worried about the death threat, and she and her boyfriend and her brother Mark took Sheesha out for the day. Due to a strange coincidence they discovered that the cruel and wicked father she was so desperately searching for, was in fact Dr Davidson himself, and the letter that had started on her voyage of hate had been nothing but lies.

'I will make it up to you for all the lonely years,' Dr Davidson promised his new-found daughter, but she realised it was too late by then – because today she had to die . . .

Chapter One

What a night to have to die! The stars that pierced the sky above their heads seemed brighter than the amber street lights, and the frost on the pavement glittered like fragments of broken glass.

'Those stars have shone out for millions of years, and will go on shining for millions more, but my life will be over in a few minutes now,' thought Sheesha bitterly. 'Sixteen years, that's all I've had. What a waste!'

Of course she knew she deserved to die. She had allowed hatred and witchcraft to control her life and deliberately set out to harm everyone in her world. Yes she certainly deserved it.

She slid her eyes sideways and peeped at Manda, striding along the deserted street beside her. Manda was the only friend she'd ever had. Something, which might have been a heart inside anyone else but Sheesha, gave a lurch. How could she have tried to destroy this one and only friend by framing her for drug pushing at school? The plan had backfired and it had been Sheesha who had been expelled from school and sent to Parkfield, a residential school for delinquent girls. Ugh! What hell that place was! When she had woken up in that dormitory this morning she had felt glad that this day had arrived at last. Why not die? There was nothing left to live for. No home, no family, no future. She even felt Manda had deserted her since that drugs business.

Yet she was frightened to die. What would it feel like, would it hurt? Her teeth were chattering again now, and cold slugs of sweat were slithering down her face. Ever since that frightful night when she had sat before her ouija board and it spelt out the fateful message that on the 14th February she would cease to exist, the date had been hanging like a rock of granite in her stomach.

'You're thinking about it again,' said Manda firmly taking her elbow. 'You're not going to die today you great wally, snap out of it.' Sheesha tried to force her stiff tense face to smile, but somehow it just would not respond. All day long it had been like this. She had not wanted to get up that morning, but had lain on her bed in the untidy dormitory after all the other girls had gone downstairs – just waiting for death. Then suddenly Manda had exploded into the room with her boyfriend and her brother, Mark.

'We're going for a day out, and we need you to make up the four,' they had said, and swept her far away from Parkfield Place, doing their best to distract her mind. It had been a wonderful day, but now the end was near, there was no escape.

'Look,' continued Manda bracingly, 'this morning you had nothing to live for, now you have everything. You've spent months trying to find your real father, and today by an extraordinary coincidence you found him. What's more he's the nicest man I've ever met, lives in a huge great house, loads of money and wants you to live there with him. You're like a princess in a fairy tale. You're going to live happily ever after. You just can't die now!'

'It's still the 14th of February,' breathed Sheesha, 'the spirits never lie.'

'That's just what they always do!' exclaimed Manda crossly. But the car was on its way towards them. They were crossing Fleetbridge High Road when they first saw its lights.

'Look out, he's drunk!' shouted Mark from the darkness ahead of them. 'Get off the road.'

But the granite block had sunk to her feet, and somehow they just would not move. Death was inevitable, so let it happen quickly. It was almost a feeling of relief that the moment had come at last.

'Don't just stand there, get out of the road,' screamed Manda and Sheesha turned her head to look at her friend for the last time. The memory of her face seared into her mind like a brand. Her frizzy ginger hair stood out from her pale face and even in the starlight you could see the freckles. Only Manda could manage freckles in February.

The car was nearly on them now, careering out of control, lurching from side to side while the tyres screeched in protest. She took a deep breath of acceptance. The spirits *had* been right. Suddenly something hit her hard in the back, sending her sprawling towards the pavement. The curb rose up and hit her bony knees while the frosty slabs came into collision with her forehead. The car never braked, it didn't even slow down, there was just a sickening thud, and then the roar of engines as it hurled away into the darkness of the open country.

'Get his number!' screamed Mark, but Manda's boyfriend Dan had something more important on his mind. Slowly it dawned on Sheesha that she was not dead. It had not been the car that had hit her – it must have been Manda who knocked her to safety. Yet the car had collided with something. She had heard that awful sound.

Bent backwards around the base of an iron lamp post, something was lying. It couldn't be human . . . could it?

'Don't move her, Dan,' warned Mark urgently. 'You can kill someone with a spinal injury if you pull them out.'

'It's too late,' sobbed Dan, 'doesn't matter what we do to her now.' But Mark was a soldier, a man of action, and leaping over a garden wall he was soon hammering on the

13

door of a nearby house. Lights split the darkness, torches flashed, a woman screamed and far away a police siren wailed eerily in the night.

'You've finally done it then,' said a grim voice from high above where Sheesha still huddled on the curbstone.

'You've tried all ways to destroy her, and now you've killed her – well done!' Mark's voice shook with rage, and his words hurt more than the impact with the car could have done.

'It was me that should have died.' Sheesha's voice rose on a note of frenzy. 'This can't have happened. She pushed me out of the way and died instead of me. I never asked her to do that! Why did it happen this way round?'

'Like a princess in a fairly tale, you'll live happily ever after.' That's what Manda had said, but could real life be like that? Certainly this bedroom did look like something out of a fairy tale. A very far cry from the dormitory at Parkfield. It was all she had ever dreamed of possessing. The sort of fluffy carpet that you sank in up to your ankles. Little cosy lamps casting pink shadows up the satiny walls. Flouncy curtains, a dainty dressing table and a business-like, well lit desk. There was even a television and an electric blanket on the bed.

Sheesha stood in the middle of the room feeling unworthy to sit down on any of the pretty chairs, let alone the silky cover on the bed.

Of course she *ought* to be happy here – years of unloving foster homes and residential care had shown her the importance of a real family and a permanent home. The man who had brought her here just an hour ago was not some 'do-gooder' offering her a home to satisfy some inner need of his own, he was her actual father, sharing the same genes and chromosomes. He had loved her since the day of her birth and for fourteen years had thought she was

14

dead. Now he wanted to make up for lost time and lavish on her everything he had – and that was a great deal.

But she had always hated men. No way would she have consented to come here and live with one, even such a nice one as this, if he had not been engaged to be married. In two months she would have a mother. All her life she had longed to have the kind of mother who would come to school functions, take care of her when she had a cold and put a hot water bottle in her bed at night. Someone she could talk to about anything.

Beth would never reject her like her last foster mother had done – or would she?

'What if she discovered everything about me?' whispered Sheesha as she stood in the middle of her Fairy Tale bedroom feeling like a dirty, slimy slug.

'She's not going to find out!' declared Sheesha out loud. 'I'm going to be so sweet and nice, she'll just never guess.'

With sudden new determination she began to unpack her few possessions, but as she moved about the room in her stiff jerky way she failed to see the smart new briefcase her father had just bought her. 'There goes another pair of tights!' she exclaimed. 'I don't look like a Fairy Tale princess and I certainly don't feel like one, and now I've even dented this case!'

She had never gone to school with her books in anything but a polythene bag so this new case was symbolic. Tomorrow she was to start at a new school, the Convent of the Sacred Heart. Picking up the damaged case she sat cradling it in her arms like an injured child. 'This is what I do to everything, mess it up!' she thought bitterly, 'I've got a chance to start a new life, but what happens if I foul it up?' 'The Convent of the Sacred Heart' had a religious ring about it. She closed her eyes and pictured rows of quiet academic girls filing into the chapel behind gliding nuns with downcast eyes. What would they say if they knew about the things she had done? She shuddered and clutched the case ever more tightly. 'At least I'll be cleverer than any of them.' She had known from her first day in infant school that she was not like other people. Teachers called her gifted, other people said she was a genius, but Sheesha felt ordinary inside. It was just that everybody she met seemed so stupid.

'I know you want to do medicine,' her father had said when he visited her at Parkfield, 'The Sacred Heart has a high academic reputation, and when you leave I'll pull strings to get you into my own college at Oxford. Your life from now on will be nothing but a blaze of success.'

'Happily ever after . . . happily ever after.' She repeated as she mechanically picked up the polythene bag that contained all her possessions and tipped them on to the floor. Out from the mass of pants and laddered tights fell a battered snapshot, and as she picked it up all her hopes of future happiness died before they had a chance to be born.

Manda last summer. Freckles extra prominent and red hair pulled into two impossible bunches. Sheesha stood looking down at it in frozen misery.

'It would have been better if you *had* died,' she whispered. Manda who had wanted to be a PE teacher and an Olympic swimmer had been flown by helicopter to the spinal injuries unit at Stoke Mandeville Hospital and they said it was unlikely she'd ever walk again.

Sheesha stood gazing down at the photo trying to think of Manda in a wheelchair.

'No!' she had shouted when her father had offered to take her to see Manda in hospital, and every time she started to write a letter she finished by tearing it up.

'It was me who should have died!' she said viciously to the photograph. 'What's the point of living here with all this if I can never be happy because of you. I deserve to suffer. You *don't*!'

A terrifying noise from downstairs made her jump and almost drop Manda's picture. It sounded like a cross between an earthquake and a thunderstorm. Was the house falling down? She wrenched open the door and ran onto the landing. At the bottom of the elegant regency staircase stood Dolly, her father's gigantic housekeeper. She was beating a bronze gong as if it were her worst enemy.

'That means it's teatime,' said the laughing voice of her father from behind her, 'I hope you're hungry.' Sheesha sprung round as a new terror filled her mind. Hungry. . . that meant food! Some people are frightened of mice, others hate spiders, but Sheesha was terrified of food. Once it had been her only comfort and she had eaten continuously until she had got so fat she had been put on a diet. Now, however, she couldn't seem to get herself off it, and she felt guilty if she swallowed anything that was not black coffee or cottage cheese.

'Dolly's been cooking all day,' continued her father, putting his hand on her shoulder. 'Feeding people is her way of showing love.' Sheesha shrank away from him – she hated to be touched, especially by men. 'What shall I do,' she though wildly, 'if they expect me to eat things like cream and chocolate cake. I'll weigh twenty stones before I can open my mouth to protest, yet I so want them to like me.' Cold sweat was trickling down her face as she followed her father into his beautiful lounge.

'Come and sit by the fire,' he said, 'you look cold.'

Every time she had been in this room, everything inside her had longed to respond to its peaceful atmosphere. The oil paintings, old furniture, soft light and gentle colours called out to her, but she was not worthy to be part of such beauty so she sat down stiffly on the edge of a Victorian chair and hoped she would not contaminate it.

'Here you are,' remarked Dolly, as she appeared behind a tea trolley positively loaded with fearsome calories.

'You're so thin a puff of wind would blow you away!' A huge smile split the folds of fat that encased her face as she poured tea from a silver pot.

'If you want more scones, just shout.' She beamed as she manoeuvred her mountain of fat out of the room.

'What will you start on?' smiled her father picking up two heaped plates. Here it was, the first confrontation. He was coming towards her holding out the food but she would have been less terrified if they had crawled with poisonous snakes and spiders. Out of her shaking hands flew the china cup spraying its contents over the velvet arm of the chair. Michael produced a large handkerchief and wiped it dry. 'We won't tell Dolly,' he smiled, 'she'd only fuss.'

'I'm so sorry,' gasped Sheesha struggling hard not to burst into tears. Michael stopped rubbing the chair and looked down into her face. Great dark eyes gazed back at him from a face so thin it looked more like a skull.

'Why are you frightened?' he asked gently. 'This is your home now, can't you just relax and enjoy it all?' They looked at each other across the wide ocean that separated them. How he had longed to have his daughter back. But had the years damaged her beyond repair?

'I've got something for you,' he said in order to break the awkward silence. 'Happy birthday!' he added as he dropped a little box into her lap.

'But it isn't my birthday,' she said nervously, 'not until September.'

'But it is the first day of the rest of your life,' he persisted. 'Mary Jenkins is dead, long live Meggan Davidson. However, I'm always going to call you Sheesha as I gave you that name the day you were born. Now, aren't you going to open the present?'

There had been so few presents in Sheesha's life that she found herself tingling all over. Inside, hidden in cotton wool lay a cross on a delicate silver chain.

18

'New life, new home, new father,' said the doctor as he looked down shyly at her tense face, 'but most important of all – new boss.'

'Boss?' she asked puzzled. 'Yes, you used to serve Satan and you wore his sign round your neck until I got Mark to break that evil stone. This cross is the sign of your new boss, Jesus Christ. He's given you this new life.' Sheesha was so absorbed in the enjoyment of it's delicate beauty that his next words came as a sudden shock.

'Don't wear it unless you really want Him to be your boss.' Sheesha sat motionless holding either end of the chain in her trembling fingers. Satan had given her great power and she had used it to get her own back on the people around her – to control them, know their secrets and cause them harm. Yet possessing that power had nearly destroyed her and in desperation she had turned to God for help. 'But I'm not fit to wear His sign round my neck – not when I killed Miss Farthing,' she thought, 'and I'm not sure I want a boss at all,' she added, as she slipped the cross into her pocket. Michael went back to his chair and buttered himself a scone. Perhaps it wasn't going to be so easy to be a father as he had always thought it would be. If only he knew what she was thinking behind that expressionless face.

The embarrassed silence was shattered as the door burst open and in swept a human whirlwind in a nurses' uniform.

'Beth!' exclaimed the doctor. 'I thought you were on duty.'

'Well,' she laughed, 'I wangled the afternoon off – after all this is rather a special day, isn't it?'

Suddenly the ordered elegance of the room was littered with discarded parts of Beth. Her coat was flung over a chair, her woolly hat and gloves on to the table, thud went her bag on the Persian carpet and parcels and packages seemed to fill every available space. Beth could never enter a room without untidying it instantly.

'Scones!' she exclaimed. 'I'm starving.' Her personality filled the whole room with warmth and Sheesha found herself wishing she could be just like Beth. Nothing ever worried her and everything made her laugh. She bounced through life like a fat round ball. 'And soon she'll be my Mum,' thought Sheesha, and found herself eating a sandwich before she realised what she was doing.

'I'll do so well at school and be so good here, I'll make them like me,' she thought, 'and soon I'll be worthy to wear that cross!'

Chapter Two

Everything began to go wrong at breakfast the very next morning.

'I'm sorry, but I can't take you to school, I must get to morning surgery,' said Michael as Dolly served boiled eggs in silver cups, and toast with the crusts cut off. Sheesha could not tell him how much it would have meant to her to swirl up to the front door of the Sacred Heart in his expensive car – walking over the muddy common just did not fit into her daydreams.

'Just go in and report to Sister Gertrude, the Head-mistress,' encouraged Michael. 'She'll be pleased to see you,' he added as he hurtled away to start his hectic day.

'*Will* she be pleased to see me?' wondered Sheesha, left alone in the elegant dining room. 'What if she had talked to Mr Atkinson, the Headmaster of Gravely, and discovered why I had been expelled?'

'But I'm gifted,' she told herself firmly. 'With brains like mine I'd be an asset to any school, and when I roar into Oxford on a cloud of brilliant exam results the old nuns will bask in reflected glory.'

Even with these encouraging thoughts to cheer her, it was still rather galling to trudge into school on foot, while rows of expensive cars, driven by expensive looking mothers disgorged expensive looking girls right onto the front doorstep, without a speck of mud on their expensive looking shoes.

'Posers!' she muttered, as she stood under the marble statue of the school founder. They streamed past her like spotless ladybirds in their red cloaks, talking to each other in high affected accents taking no more notice of her than they did of the statue above her head.

'Come on!' she told herself, 'psyche yourself up! they're no better than you are now, no richer, and not nearly so clever. You could talk in that ridiculous way too if you wanted to.' She'd never had a single friend in all her school career except for Manda, but surely that had only been because she had always been the 'girl from the children's home', or the foster child in the secondhand uniform. All that had changed now. She would make lots of friends here. . . so long as they never found out about . . .

Sister Gertrude, said the sign on the door, and Sheesha pictured an elderly nun with a wrinkled, serene face smiling at her from the folds of a dazzling white wimple while she welcomed her kindly to the school. But something was wrong. There was no way of knowing that Sister Gertrude was a nun except than she wore a large cross on her porridge coloured jumper. She was also young, unsmiling and looked rather cross. She continued to shuffle through the papers on her desk and she did not even look up when Sheesha walked into the room. Neither did she ask her to sit down, so Sheesha sat down anyway by way of protest.

'They're lucky to have me,' she told herself firmly. 'She can't know who I am, that's all.'

But even that hope was dashed when Sister Gertrude screwed the top on her pen and said, 'so you are the "gel" from Parkfield.'

If she had thrown a bucket of iced water over her, Sheesha could not have been more shocked. This was certainly *not* the image she wanted to project.

'I was only there a few weeks,' she protested, 'I was at Gravely before that.'

22

'Quite!' said Sister Gertrude and her tone made it perfectly clear that she considered the comprehensive only one stage better than the detention centre.

'You will be a long way behind our "gels" I'm afraid, how old are you?'

'Sixteen and a half!' gasped Sheesha.

'Regrettable,' commented the nun, 'dreadful time to change schools. Well, you can't take your exams this summer, that is quite certain. You will have to wait down in the fifth form for an extra year. Now go to room 26 – just down the corridor.'

'But I can't!' exploded Sheesha.

'Why not, it is your Form room.'

'Not the room,' said Sheesha impatiently, 'I mean I can't waste a whole year.' Sister Gertrude was not used to being spoken to like this by "gels" and she put on her glasses to take a closer look at this odd specimen.

'You don't understand,' exploded Sheesha, 'I'm gifted. I could have got A grades in all these exams if I'd taken them two years ago!'

Sister Gertrude slowly wiped the steam from her glasses. 'We are not used to taking in delinquents,' she said at last. 'I did it in your case because I respect your father, but I am beginning to think I made an error of judgement. . . and one thing more,' she added coldly, as she turned back to her papers, 'don't mention Parkfield to any of the other "gels" will you – we don't want that kind of thing getting back to the parents.'

'Shall I say I've just come from Roedean?' enquired Sheesha sweetly.

'There is never any need to lie,' said Sister Gertrude icily, and she lifted her hand in gracious dismissal.

Ever since the first day in infant school when she had bitten the teacher, anger had been Sheesha's defence, but also her downfall. She could feel it rising in her now,

23

demanding that she had the last word, and it would not have been a polite one.

'I'm going to be different now,' she told herself as she bit her tongue and managed not to slam the door. Yet she was shaking with rage as she walked towards room 26.

After life in a large comprehensive and then a reform school she expected to see heads bent studiously over books in this hot-house for religious academics, but yet another shock was in store for Sheesha as she stood in the doorway of her new form room. The teacher had been delayed, so the occupants were all sitting on their desks talking at the tops of their voices as they restyled each other's hair or varnished their finger nails.

'Who on earth are you?' demanded a girl with severe acne as the conversation evaporated and they all turned to stare.

'It's only a telegraph pole,' giggled another voice.

'No it's an underweight daddy-long-legs,' put in a girl with a brace on her teeth. At six feet two and weighing only seven stone, Sheesha did look rather less than human, but the comments did nothing to improve her temper.

'Name?' demanded the spotty girl.

'I'm Mary Jenkins,' she began and then clapped her hand over her mouth in horror. 'No, I mean Meggan Davidson.' She had done the one thing she had been most frightened of doing and her armpits prickled with embarrassment. It is as difficult to change your name as it is to change your personality.

'Make up your mind,' sneered the girl with the brace, 'sure you're not Princess Diana?'

'What school were you at before?' asked a voice from the back of the room. Here it was, the question she had dreaded. Sheesha looked round at their scornful faces, noted their fashionable hairstyles and beautiful clothes and said, 'Roedean' without a second thought.

'I was there until last year,' came the inevitable voice, 'but I don't remember you.'

'I've lost weight,' stammered Sheesha prickling again, 'and I've grown a lot.' In her agitation her carefully practiced accent was slipping into a Parkfield drawl and she hated herself for it.

'Have you got a horse?' asked a weather beaten girl with a well-developed backside.

'Two,' lied Sheesha desperately.

'Really?' said the girl almost sounding friendly, 'do you jump them?' The only encounter Sheesha had ever had with a horse was when one had bitten her during a primary school visit to a zoo so she was highly relieved when the teacher pattered in.

'Could this silly little round woman really be a nun too?' thought Sheesha incredulously.

'Oh, you are the new girl from Parkfield,' she twittered and then added with a flutter of agitation, 'Oh dear, I wasn't supposed to say that was I?'

'She looks far more like the sort of thing who'd come from a place like Parkfield,' sneered the girl who had once been to Roedean. 'We don't really want her sort here.'

'I bet you don't know a showjumper from a seaside donkey,' added the girl with the large backside.

At Parkfield, if someone needled you, you blacked their eye, instead of hissing like a pedigree cat. If this was what being rich and well-bred did for you, Sheesha almost wished she was back there again.

Her smouldering anger was reaching a dangerous level, and the little nun was about to light the final fatal match.

'Now now, Lower Fifth, let's calm down.'

'*Lower* Fifth!' gasped Sheesha, realising she had reached explosion point. 'If this is the *Lower* Fifth, I'm in the wrong class. I'm sixteen!'

'Yes dear,' soothed the fat little sparrow, 'but we've got a lot of catching up to do haven't we?'

'No we haven't!' shouted Sheesha, standing up with such force that her chair crashed to the floor behind her.

'I'll take my exams this summer without any stupid school! You don't want me, and I certainly don't want you, so I'm getting out.' Seizing her battered briefcase she jerked herself to the door and this time slammed it with devastating force. . . and enjoyed doing so.

'I must see Doctor Davidson at once,' demanded Sheesha, as ten minutes later she burst into the crowded surgery, positively shoving two old ladies out of her path.

'That is quite impossible without an appointment,' said the receptionist coldly.

'But I'm his daughter,' spat Sheesha.

'Really?' said the receptionist looking her up and down in surprise, 'well in that case you had better go in now, a patient has just come out.'

'Sheesha!' exclaimed the Doctor starting up from behind his desk in surprise. 'I was expecting an old man with Parkinson's disease.'

'I'm never going back to that dump of a school!' shouted Sheesha without wasting time on preliminaries. 'It's full of horse-riding cows!'

'The mind boggles!' said the doctor trying hard not to laugh.

'You're just the same as all men,' bellowed Sheesha, 'you just can't take anything seriously.'

'I'm sorry,' replied her father meekly. Whatever had happened to the silent girl who never volunteered a remark and only answered him in monosyllables? How was an old widower like him ever going to cope with a fiery dragon like this, who changed personalities as easily as she changed her clothes?

A tentative knock on the door relieved the tension. 'That will be my Parkinson's,' said Michael, 'you sit in the waiting room until I'm through with this lot, then we'll talk this out over a coffee.'

'I don't want any coffee,' growled Sheesha.

'Have tea then,' said her father as he propelled her towards the door. 'I've got a whole room full of people out there with real problems.'

'I'm not budging from here until you do something,' shouted Sheesha as she collided with the shaky old patient in the doorway. Every head in the waiting room turned in astonishment, the three secretaries glared through their glass window and a district nurse stuck an incredulous head round a consulting room door.

'What's so interesting?' demanded Sheesha rudely and flopped down on a plastic chair to lie in wait for her father.

Almost at once the door of Michael's consulting room burst open and out dashed the doctor himself hitching on his overcoat as he ran by his astonished patients.

'Sorry!' he shouted, 'I've been called out on an emergency!' and was out of the front door without a backward look.

'He's not getting away from me like that!' thought Sheesha and sprang after him. He said nothing as she dived into the passenger seat, and she was beginning to think he had not noticed her until he said suddenly, 'Do your seat belt up, I'm going to have to break the speed limit.'

And he most certainly did. Sheesha would never have belived it possible to get from one side of Fleetbridge to the other so quickly. She felt she was in an American police drama.

'Typical of a man!' she thought scornfully, 'they never grow out of playing cars.'

27

With a squeal of protest from the brakes they pulled up in front of the neat little semi on the outskirts of town, and the front door opened as soon as his feet pounded the path. Sheesha followed him into the house despising him, but her attitude towards him soon changed dramatically.

'Come in the sittingroom, Doctor,' said a tearful little woman, who seemd as unaware of Sheesha as Michael was himself. A man was lying on the sofa gasping for breath, his face as white as his clean shirt.

As she stood spellbound by the door, Sheesha watched her father with mounting admiration. Deft speed, coupled with professional calm – he was magnificent! 'How much you have to know to save a life,' she thought as she watched him plunge the hypodermic into the heaving chest.

'Massive myocardial infarction,' he remarked to her over his shoulder, 'ring and get an ambulance will you Sheesha?' Silently she noted the reassuring way he spoke to his patient, his gentleness with the man's wife and his detached professionalism when he talked to the hospital on the phone.

'See how fast this bus will go,' he told the ambulance men as they finally lifted the stretcher. 'You go along with your husband, Mrs Porter, I'll see the house is locked up.'

'He would have died, wouldn't he, if you hadn't got here in time,' said Sheesha as they watched the blue flashing light disappear round the corner.

'He might have lasted another minute or so,' said her father calmly, 'but that's all part of the routine when you are a GP.' All her anger was gone, and in its place two other emotions were grappling for supremacy. A deep admiration for this man who was actually her father and a stronger than ever desire to be a doctor herself one day.

Two hours later her convictions were just as strong, but her feet were killing her. 'I'm taking you on my rounds,' Michael had said when they returned to the surgery to find all the patients had evaporated. She had never experienced anything so exhausting. Up and down staircases, farm tracks and garden paths they had hurtled, constantly adjusting to a new situation.

'How does he do it?' Sheesha wondered, 'with some patients he jokes, with others he's sympathetic, he's cross with one and endlessly patient with the next. How does he know what each one needs?' Once long ago he had told her that he prayed before seeing each patient. Did God give him power to adapt so remarkably? Did he heal through God's power just as surely as she had once harmed through Satan's?

'You'd better stay in the car this time,' Michael's voice cut into her thoughts and made her jump. 'The patient is a teenager with emotional problems.' 'Dad's like a video perpetually on fast forward,' Sheesha thought as she watched her father disappear in a figurative cloud of dust, and tipping back her seat she closed her eyes. A velvety cloak of weakness settled over her. She knew it was lack of food but the sensation was rather pleasant, 'and its cheaper than drugs and glue,' she thought sleepily.

'God will never give *you* the power to be a great doctor.' Sheesha shot bolt upright and the seat belt cut into her flat chest. The voice had come from inside her head and it was sickeningly familiar. She had heard it often when she had been controlled by Satan.

'I don't belong to you now!' she said to the great surprise of a woman who was walking along the pavement.

'You don't belong to anyone, so why shouldn't I have you back?' continued the voice. 'You're no good to God with a past like yours.' Faces began to waft towards her out of her memory, faces of people she had hurt.

'You couldn't even survive in that school for half an hour without causing a riot – you're useless.'

'No!' sobbed Sheesha, 'I won't listen to you.'

29

'Come back to me and let me give you power again, you're just nothing on your own.'

The car door opened and her father slid under the steering wheel. Everything inside Sheesha longed to reach out to him and ask him for his help, but she had let him see her angry and abusive. He wouldn't want to love her now. Earlier she had been so infuriated she had not cared what he thought of her – now she minded intensely.

'Poor lass,' he said gently, and for one wonderful moment Sheesha thought he meant her. 'Poor lass,' he continued, 'she's an intelligent kid, but she's got a huge school phobia and now she's developed agoraphobia as well. She just can't go out of the house. I've got her a peripatetic teacher and she's working hard at home, but . . .'

'Couldn't I have one?' cut in Sheesha.

'Have what?' asked Michael blankly as he started the engine.

'A peripatetic teacher. I could easily work at home.'

Michael said nothing as he eased the car into the busy Fleetbridge High Street, then suddenly he asked, 'When did you last eat?'

Taken completely by surprise Sheesha stammered, 'I was a bit too excited for breakfast.'

'And supper last night,' he added, 'so I'm taking you to the Copper Kettle for lunch. No one can cope with horse-riding cows on an empty stomach.'

He ordered home-made steak pie and then smiled at her over the polished table.

'Well, you've sampled the life of a GP this morning. Will that be your field or are you going to be one of the big noises in hospital?'

'I've always wanted to be a gynaecologist,' admitted Sheesha, 'but I don't think I really care, so long as it's in medicine.

'You'll never make it with a peripatetic teacher,' said her father softly.

'Why not?' demanded Sheesha, 'I've got enough brains to get brilliant results without any silly school.'

'Medicine is desperately hard to get into,' said her father gently. 'They don't just want academic achievement, they'll need a first class school report too.'

Once again Sheesha used anger as her defence, 'It's not my fault if I'm like I am,' she blazed, 'I've had a difficult life.'

'Are you going to go on blaming that for all your problems?' he asked mildly.

'I might as well die now, if I can't do medicine,' replied Sheesha simply. 'There's nothing else worth doing.'

Michael looked across at her and suddenly the ocean that separated them the previous day seemed very much narrower.

'I feel like that too,' he said gently, and as their eyes met across the steaming plates of food a new understanding began to grow between them.

'You're so like me,' he whispered absently.

Sheesha picked up her fork and began to push a piece of potato round her plate. 'I always seem to foul things up,' she said, desperately hoping that he would understand.

'Jesus actually died to cut you off from the effects of your past life. Don't forget he took the punishment for all the bad things you did – but he also wants to heal all the horrible memories you have stored up in your head and He'll give you the power to be a different person.'

'I can't sit back and let Him do all that,' said Sheesha heavily, 'and I'm sorry, I just can't eat this food either.'

'It's my half day,' said Michael, 'no more patients, lets go for a drive.' Without waiting for a response he rushed off to pay for the meal they had not eaten and ignoring the astonished expression on the waitress's face he lead her out of the cafe.

'Where are we going?' asked Sheesha nervously.

'Just to lay a ghost,' he replied and unlocked the car door.

Her mind told her it was some hours later. She must have been asleep before they left Fleetbridge, worn out by lack of food and excitement. But wherever were they now? Sheesha peered out of the window and cold horror enveloped her. 'Stoke Mandeville, Spinal Injuries Unit', said a green hospital sign.

'No! You know I can't face Manda! You must have drugged my coffee to get me here!'

Michael parked the car, and prayed earnestly under his breath. They were both used to imposing their own will on other people. One had used the force of her personality, the other had used charm, but they had both usually succeeded. Now they eyed each other like a couple of boxers before the first round.

'I can't drag you in there by the hair, screaming and kicking, can I?' he said helplessly. 'You'll have to face her one day, so why not now? Come on, a doctor's life is made up of difficulties.'

'I must make him like me,' thought Sheesha as slowly and unwillingly she followed him into the building. He was right of course – she wouldn't be able to cope with life until this was over.

At any other time she would have been fascinated to visit an internationally famous hospital like this. She would have plied her father with questions about procedures and techniques and the role of the physiotherapist but she realised for the first time that it was easy to take a detached clinical interest in patients until you actually happened to know them – and Manda was here instead of her.

Her frizzy red hair was just the same, but that was all.

That shrunken white face couldn't belong to Manda! And the body clamped into traction, still and lifeless, that wasn't Manda's either.

She left Michael to do all the talking while she sat on the edge of her chair twisting her hankie into a sweaty piece of string. They tried hard to include her in their conversation, chatting about the other patients, the handsome doctors and the fussy staff nurse, the food and long nights – all the things hospital patients always talk about, but all Sheesha could do was gaze at the drawn little face and struggle not to let herself be sick.

At last Michael said, 'I'm just going to pull rank on the sister, and ask her how long you'll be in traction,' and he was off up the ward leaving them alone to face each other at last.

'Hello,' said Manda softly. 'How's it going?' Sheesha could not think of a reply, so she made none.

'Is that your new school uniform?' tried Manda again . . .

'It's my *old* school uniform,' barked Sheesha. 'I left the place this morning.

'They haven't kicked you out already?' said Manda in horror.

'No, I walked, or rather ran out – load of silly cows!'

'How about the fairy tale?' said Manda.

'Fairy tale?' repeated Sheesha blankly.

'You know, being rich and having a home and family, you always said you'd be happy if you had all that.'

That was too much, the tension inside Sheesha suddenly snapped and she gasped, 'Happy! How could I ever be happy with you here like this?'

There was a tense silence then a flush began to spread over Manda's face and extend down her thin neck. A danger signal and Sheesha read it at once. Soon her eyes would begin to turn dark and flash with fury, Manda was going into one of her rages. Instinctively Sheesha pushed the chair back from the bed. Too well she remembered that in one such rage Manda had clawed her face like an angry tiger. Some of the scars were still there. But how could this captive body express its emotions now? Could Manda's rage be confined to words? Apparently it could, because she took a deep breath and began.

'How dare you say that! I didn't have to be here you know. When I saw that car coming I began to run for safety, then I saw you standing there in the road – just asking for death, because you believed it was inevitable. Didn't you realise I did it deliberately?' She wasn't shouting. Her voice hissed like an angry snake.

'Oh I thought I'd get out of the way as well, when I pushed you. I didn't really expect to be hit, but I was willing to risk it. And why? Because I wanted you to be happy. I couldn't bear you to die on the very day you had been given everything you ever wanted. Now you have the gall to sit there and tell me you've walked out of school and you're not happy. All this ghastly horror would *almost* be bearable if I thought I had achieved something worthwhile. Now you tell me it was all a waste.'

Sheesha shifted uneasily in her moulded plastic chair. Manda was so angry she might do herself some kind of harm.

'You know what's the matter with you!' continued Manda relentlessly. 'You don't want to be happy! You're only happy if you are miserable. You just were not worth a cut finger, let alone a broken back!' Her voice was rising out of control now, and it finished as a shout.

'You let me do this for nothing!'

Wheelchairs spun round, visitors turned to look and nurses peered round curtains. Sister hurried out of her glass fronted office followed closely by Michael.

'Nurse – screens,' snapped Sister, for Manda was crying now and so was Sheesha.

'I think it's time we left,' said Michael, 'but we will come back soon, Manda.'

'Don't bother,' hiccupped Manda looking at Sheesha fixedly. 'Don't bother to come back. Unless you accept it and let yourself be happy, I don't ever want to see you again.' Sister hustled them down the ward and with Sheesha still crying they got silently into the car. Michael said nothing until they were on the open road, then he spoke.

'That's two people who've given up everything to make you happy.'

'Two?' faltered Sheesha.

'Yes, Jesus died for you and Manda very nearly did.'

'But I didn't *ask* either of them to,' stormed Sheesha. 'It just makes me feel bad. *I* ought to suffer for my own mess.'

'But they don't want you to feel bad, they wanted to make you happy. Why don't you accept what they did for you and start living?'

'I *am* living!' protested Sheesha.

'No you're not,' said her father, 'if you don't start eating soon you'll kill yourself, do you know that? A lot of anorexics do, you know. Go back to school, work on Sister Gertrude until you have her eating out of your hand. You're a great actress, act the part of a horse-riding cow – I'll buy you a horse if it would help! Stop cowering away from life – attack it!'

'They'd never have me back after this mnorning,' sobbed Sheesha, 'I blew it.'

'I'll talk to Sister Gertrude this evening,' promised Michael, 'and look – Motorway Services – let's get some food into you.'

Life or death lay on a plate before her, disguised as beefburgers and chips. 'If I dig my fork in and start eating, I'm saying yes to life,' she thought.

Suddenly the memory of Manda's white face seemed to look up at her. 'It really matters to her that I'm happy,' she thought.

'I'll eat the burgers but not the chips,' she announced firmly. 'I'll accept what Manda did, but I'm not worthy of Jesus Christ yet.'

'You'll never be worthy of His love,' replied Michael gently, 'but then, none of us ever are. Come on, eat the burgers, they'll be a start in the right direction.'

'Well dear, I really have to admit your work is exceptional.' It was a very different Sister Gertrude who faced Sheesha across her desk seven days later. She had reluctantly agreed to give the 'gel' one more chance, and had given her past exam papers in all ten of her subjects to work through in the library. After looking at them she had sat for some ten minutes in silent wonder. Never had the Sacred Heart been blessed by a pupil with a mind like this.

'It would be rather a pity to wait a year for your exams,' she continued as she actually smiled graciously at Sheesha. 'We'll put you straight into the upper fifth.' A thrill of triumph ran through Sheesha, but she forced herself to play the part of the demure convent girl. If her future depended on this silly little woman, then act she could.

'I'm very sorry about that first day, Sister Gertrude, I think I was just a bit tense,' she stammered with downcast eyes.

Sister Gertrude looked mollified. 'I think we both managed each other badly, dear,' she said. 'Humour the "gel",' she added under her breath. 'She could do the academic reputation of the school nothing but good.'

The upper fifth were a better looking lot than room 26 had been. The pressure of their exams only three months away occupied their minds wonderfully. But after less than a week Sheesha had abandoned the hope that they might be friendly. They had all formed into their little cliques and were profoundly disinterested in anyone who had neither good looks, a bubbly personality or the ability to play netball. But at least they allowed Sheesha to merge into the background unmolested.

'Who cares!' thought Sheesha viciously. 'They're a brainless lot anyway.' As the days went by, however, she began to realise that was not true. For the first time in all her school life she became aware of someone else in the class whose intelligence was almost equal to her own, and she was intrigued. Pippa was the natural star of the class and had been, all the way up the school. She stood out from everyone else in the Upper Fifth with her long blonde hair and wide smiling face. But it was not her looks or her laugh that impressed Sheesha. 'She's got the kind of mind I could actually communicate with,' she thought, 'but she'd never want to talk to me.'

It was quite an ordinary book, in fact it looked positively dull as it stood on the shelf in the biology section of the school library, but two hands reached out towards it at exactly the same moment.

'I got it first!'

'No, I did, and I've got to have it tonight for that essay!'

'But I've got to do the essay too, remember!' The old nun who was the librarian hobbled over to the two antagonists waving her arms in frail protest.

'Girls, girls, remember the rule of silence, this is the library! Who had the book first?'

'We've been set an essay,' smiled Pippa regaining her usual calm. 'This is the only source book on the topic and we both got here at the same time.'

'But I *must* have it tonight,' put in Sheesha, 'I've got so much to catch up on.'

'Look,' said Pippa, 'I read so fast, I'll have this finished by eight this evening. I'll bring it round to you then. I know where you live, your Dad's our doctor.' Sheesha was so pleased to meet someone else who could read a book as quickly as she could herself, that she found herself smiling.

'Thanks,' she said, 'that's nice of you.'

'Pippa can usually be depended on to keep the peace,' said the old librarian, shooting a look of dislike at Sheesha as she hobbled back to her desk.

Michael was out at a church meeting that evening and Dolly was at Bingo, so when the bell rang, it was Sheesha who ran downstairs to open the door.

'Can I come in?' asked Pippa. 'I heard someone say you wanted to be a doctor, and I've never met anyone else who wanted to be one too.'

'You're going to do medicine?' exclaimed Sheesha.

'Never wanted to do anything else,' smiled Pippa. An hour later Sheesha had to pinch herself hard in case this was just a lovely dream. Sitting either end of her bed they had talked non-stop and still were only scratching the surface of one another's minds.

'Life really would be great,' thought Sheesha as she waved Pippa goodbye, 'if I had a friend like that. But will she want to know me back at Snob House?'

It seemed that she did, for the next morning when the bell rang for break, Sheesha found herself seized by the elbow and propelled into the fifth year common room before she had a chance to escape to the loos, which was where she usually took refuge.

'Which college did you say you wanted to try for in Oxford?' began Pippa, as she offered Sheesha a bite of her Mars Bar.

'You've taken on another lame dog have you, Pippa?' drawled an unpleasant voice from behind them. 'I'm surprised at you, letting a girl like that share your Mars, you might catch something nasty.'

'Don't take any notice of Amy,' smiled Pippa, turning her back on the unpleasant sneering face of the class creep.

'Perhaps you're trying to convert her,' continued Amy relentlessly. 'Going to drag her off to that ridiculous church of yours?'

'I don't suppose I'll have to drag her there,' countered Pippa. 'Her father's one of the deacons. You must be very proud of him,' she added turning back to Sheesha, 'everyone looks up to him. I've only just discovered religion and I'd give anything for my parents to be into it with me.'

The rest of the day shot by as their friendship deepened, and Sheesha just could not remember a nicer school day.

'See you on Sunday morning,' called Pippa when they parted at the school gate, 'going to that church is a terrific experience. You wait and see!'

'I don't know why I bother cooking for you two,' grumbled Dolly as she stamped into the dining room at breakfast time on Sunday morning. Michael and Sheesha both sat with their books propped up in front of them, reading in companionable silence as they did during every meal. 'You can't taste a bite, poring over them books.'

Dumping a plate of bacon and eggs in front of Michael, she left the room with a sniff of disgust.

Michael looked anxiously at his daughter who was toying with a piece of dry toast while savouring a book on microbiology. 'How can I put it to her?' he thought. 'She'll never say yes.' If only this strange girl with her lightning changes of mood, fears and tensions, could find the stability that he had discovered by knowing God. But how would she react if he asked her to go with him to church?

Suddenly Sheesha closed her book with a snap, and said, 'I'm coming with you this morning, so I'd better go and tog myself up.' Because she dashed out of the room so quickly, she missed the look of surprise and pleasure that crossed her father's face.

'I must be mad!' she thought half an hour later as they turned into the crowded church car park. 'Me going to church!' She had only done it in order to please Pippa and her father, the two most important people in her life at the moment, but she was beginning to feel she had made a huge mistake.

'There'll be loads of other young people there,' smiled her father, 'you'll love it.' But he was very wrong! She hated it from the moment she stepped throught the door, for someone who knew nothing about churches she had very fixed ideas about what they should be like. A handful of people in rigid pews listening with bowed heads while choir boys performed ethereal music to the ancient rafters. But this church was not like that. It was crammed with people, talking, laughing and waving to each other across the aisle. The building was large and new. 'Like a cinema with windows,' thought Sheesha in disgust, and there was no sign of Pippa in the heaving throng.

'Can't we sit at the back?' she pleaded, but there was no room, and they had no choice but to walk to the front. Sheesha recognized many faces from Gravely, and she began to wish she could fall into an old-fashioned vault and be entombed forever. Curious glances shot towards her from all over the church and people exchanged whispered comments with their neighbours. It was only natural, after all, when someone with the reputation for witchcraft arrives at church. They were genuinely glad to see her, but it was too much for Sheesha. 'I can't stay here,' she whispered to Michael, 'I'm off.'

'Give it a try,' he pleaded, but she shook off his restraining hand and darted back up the church. Heads turned and eyes followed her along the aisle, but she did not stop running until she was in the fresh air. 'I would have choked if I'd stayed in there,' she thought, as the feeling of suffocation began to recede. 'Those people are too close to God for my comfort.'

As she began to walk away from the unpleasant church she suddenly became conscious that someone was following her. The feet were too light to be her father's, she thought, so she quickened her pace.

'Meggan, wait,' protested a voice with a familiar ring. 'Oh, no,' she thought as she wheeled around to face Pippa. 'All the Gravely people will have told her about me, and so she'll never want to be my friend.'

'Why are you running away?' demanded Pippa, 'I was so pleased to see you come in. No one else from our class goes to that church.'

'I didn't like it,' replied Sheesha stiffly. 'I like traditional churches better.'

'I bet you have never been in any sort of church before,' panted Pippa. 'You used to be a witch, didn't you?'

'So you know,' gasped Sheesha, and suddenly burst into tears.

Pippa took her firmly by the arm and pushed her down onto a seat that overlooked the famous Fleetbridge Common.

'I don't know anything about you,' she said, 'but when you came in with your Dad some of my friends whispered that you'd been into witchcraft, and it's all over the school that you were once at Parkfield.'

'And tomorrow morning you'll tell them why, and then their smug little Mums and Dads will lean on Sister Gertrude to get me expelled,' sobbed Sheesha.

'But you're not a witch now, are you?' persisted Pippa. 'Does that mean you've become a Christian?'

'I don't belong to Satan any more,' growled Sheesha, 'but I'm not ready to open myself up to God yet either. I'm just empty.'

41

'D'you know what started me wanting to be a doctor?' asked Pippa unexpectedly. 'It was my great aunt Janice. She lives in an old people's home near the Parish Church. She's a doctor, or was. She's over ninety now, but she's the most wonderful person I know. She told me once that God gives us enormous powers to do good, just as Satan gives us enormous powers to do harm. I suppose when you belonged to him, that's what he used you for.'

Sheesha sat looking at Pippa for a long time. If only she dared tell this girl some of the things that no other human being knew. Satan had indeed given her great power, and what terrible havoc he had caused through her. But she wanted this girl as a friend too badly to risk losing her.

'Why won't you let God work through you?' continued Pippa. 'You won't be much good on your own.'

'Give me time,' replied Sheesha, 'I've got all the rest of my life, we've got years to talk about all this.'

For months Sheesha could never pass that seat by the Common without bitterly regretting those words. Time to talk with Pippa was something she just did not have.

Chapter Three

'Where on earth are you taking me?' protested Sheesha, 'I've got a load of work I should be doing.'

It was the following Saturday morning and Pippa had dragged Sheesha from the security of her desk insisting that she must come on a mystery expedition. It was the last thing Sheesha wanted to do, but Pippa had been so friendly at school all the week she felt she owed her a favour. She had never once mentioned witchcraft or religion – she was a friend worth having.

All the same she was beginning to prickle all over with apprehension when she realized they were walking right into the estate where she had once lived with Manda. She certainly did not want to bump into someone who remembered her, and might smash her new carefully created image.

Pippa was making for the Old Parish Church that stood among the modern houses looking pathetically out of place. She and Manda had spent so many hours under the yew trees in the churchyard, talking to the funny little old lady who so often sat there, that a nostalgic lump appeared in Sheesha's throat.

'You're going to meet my great aunt Janice,' whispered Pippa as they approached the church porch. 'You'll love her.'

'Sherbet lemons!' exclaimed Sheesha stopping dead in her tracks with surprise. There sitting in the porch surrounded by rugs sat the little old lady who she remembered so well. They had called her 'our old lady', and enjoyed the sherbet sweets she always had in her handbag.

'How lovely to see you again, my dear,' quavered the old voice. 'I've prayed so often for you.'

'So you two already know each other,' laughed Pippa. 'We've come to pick your brains about medicine in the old days, Auntie, my friend here wants to be a doctor too.'

Most old people moan about their ailments, but great aunt Janice was different. Soon she had the girls talking about their ambitions, hopes and ideas, leading them on by a series of penetrating questions. Sheesha thought she had never met a more interesting person.

'What branch of medicine interested you?' she asked the old doctor as the Spring morning trickled happily away.

'I had to be an all-rounder, my dear. You see as soon as I qualified I went out as a missionary doctor up into Northern India. Then I spent years tramping round Tibet with my two assistants.'

'Why didn't you just become a GP in this country?' asked Sheesha curiously.

'I wanted those people to know God loved them enough to die for them and of course there was no proper medical care out there in those days. Our patients didn't come to us, we had to tramp round mountain villages and forgotten valleys looking for them. It was very dangerous sometimes.'

'Why?' laughed Sheesha. 'Because of the Abominable Snowman?'

'No, it was bandits that were our nightmare,' smiled the old Doctor. 'We were camped one night in our goatskin tents, just three English women alone in the mountains, when I woke up and heard people prowling about in the darkness outside.'

44

'Surely you had native bearers to carry your equipment,' put in Sheesha.

'We did, but they ran for their lives. These men were quite ruthless and were delighted to have three young women in their power. I can assure you, my dear, we faced a fate worse than death, followed by death itself.'

'What happened then?' asked Pippa.

'They all came pushing into our tent and an uglier bunch of men would be hard to find as they waved their knives at us. Then I felt the power of God coming down on me.' She smiled. 'I had no knowledge of their language, but God gave me the power to speak in their dialect, and I said, "You cannot touch us, we belong to God and He will not permit it." One by one their eyes fell and they shuffled away out of the tent and we never saw them again.'

'I didn't know that God could give power like that!' exclaimed Sheesha, fascinated.

'Oh yes,' said the old doctor, 'he gives us all the power we need, but sometimes we like to manage on our own without him, and that's when we fail. I'm finding it much harder to use His power now than ever I did out in Tibet.'

'Surely there aren't bandits in Fleetbridge?' laughed Pippa.

'My dear,' smiled the old lady, 'I live with fifteen other old ladies, and I can assure you they are often much harder to live with than bandits. God will give us the power to love the irritating poeple we live with, but so often we are so cross with them we won't ask for it!'

'I won't need that kind of power,' thought Sheesha happily, 'not living with people like Dad and Beth, they'd never irritate me.'

'I must get home,' smiled Aunt Janice, 'or Matron will be cross with me again. Have another sherbet lemon, my dears, before I go.'

Sheesha looked back on those first two months in her new home as the lull before the storm. She had once possessed the gift of seeing into the future. She would certainly not have been so happy if she had still possessed that gift. School was a positive delight with Pippa as a friend, and they spent most of their Saturday mornings with her Aunt Janice, talking endlessly about the changes in medical practice. Life with Dolly was more like living in a five star hotel, and the more she saw of her father the more she liked him, and soon she was taking her homework down to the lounge in the evenings and doing it on the rug by the fire with her father reading beside her. They both liked exactly the same kind of music and it was so refreshing to be with someone who never broke into your chain of thought by making silly remarks.

They were sitting like this one evening when Beth bounced into the room. She didn't walk, she literally bounced.

'I'm going to buy my wedding dress on Saturday,' she announced. 'Come with me Sheesha, and help me choose.' Sheesha felt deeply pleased. 'Just to think – she actually wants me!' she thought happily, but Beth's next words chilled her to the bone.

'I'd love you to be my bridesmaid.'

'Oh no!' gasped Sheesha in horror, 'that's not my scene. Frilly dresses and flowers in the hair, it's not me at all!' The very thought of standing up there in church with everyone thinking how tall and ugly she was filled her with dread. 'Please don't make me!' she added appealingly.

'I just thought you'd like it,' laughed Beth, 'but it doesn't matter.'

Saturday was not quite the success that Sheesha had expected it to be. After a long morning watching Beth trying to squeeze her size 16 middle-aged body into dresses designed for size 12 teenagers, she was exhausted. Beth, however, was quite unruffled and proceeded to eat three cream eclairs for her lunch in the nearest cafe. 'Life's too short to diet,' she laughed. 'I'll buy some material and run the thing up in my size.' Beth had woken that morning right in the middle of a wonderful dream, and as she sat there munching her last cream cake, she allowed herself to slip back into the atmosphere of it. She and Michael had been sitting on his sofa with several babies crawling all over them eating jam doughnuts. Neither in a dream or out of it would it have mattered to Beth if gooey jam and sticky sugar got onto the velvet cushions, so it was just as well that Dolly had not been included in the dream. All her life Beth had longed for a baby. As a young staff nurse she had worked on a children's ward, until the desperate longing for a baby of her own had become too strong to handle, and she had transferred into psychiatric work. As the years had rolled by, the longing had not lessened and she buried the grief behind a smiling face. Now at last her dream could come true, after all, even at forty there was still time for several babies.

'Would your daughter like another cake, Madam?' The voice of the waitress jarred her back into the world of reality.

'No thanks,' said Sheesha firmly, while the words 'your daughter' vibrated in Beth's ears. 'In three weeks I'll be a mother,' she thought. 'I won't have to wait for a doughnut eating baby.' She looked across the table at Sheesha and some of her happiness trickled away. Any other teenage daughter might have been a gift from Heaven, but why had God given her the only girl she had never really understood? She had a brilliant reputation for handling difficult young patients, her student nurses adored her and the young people at church all told her their troubles, but could she ever handle this girl with her expressionless face and intimidating brains? 'I'll just have to teach her to laugh and enjoy life a bit more,' she told herself, but somehow Sheesha sitting stiff and tense at the other side of the table just did not fit into her dream of babies and doughnuts, and it took Beth a supreme effort to put the smile back onto her face.

'Your daughter'. The words were echoing in Sheesha's ears as well, and behind her frozen face she was hugging herself with joy. 'When she's my mum I'll have everything in the world I've always wanted, a great school, a special friend, mother and father, money and a future in medicine. I'll write to Manda tonight and tell her I'm beginning to live happily ever after at last.'

It was panic that woke her. Something was going to go wrong, the certainty felt like a grave-stone pushing her down through the mattress.

'It can't last,' she thought, struggling out of sleep. 'This happiness can't last – it never does for me.' She sat up in bed fixing her attention on the familiar objects about her and telling herself not to be so stupid. The sun was streaming in through the chinks in the curtains and it was April 26th, the day of the wedding. They had all looked forward to this day so much, but now it had come she suddenly didn't feel she could face it. It had been a strange week, every moment she had spent with her father had felt precious, as if everything was coming to an end, and however much she told herself that having Beth around would only make things even nicer, she had not been able to quell a mounting feeling of anxiety. Pippa had been away from school all week, and no one seemed to know why, and Amy had made it her personal business to be as mean as possible to Sheesha who felt desperately vulnerable without Pippa's protection.

Dolly had been in a vile mood because after the honeymoon she was leaving to live with her sister on the far side of Fleetbridge and she hated the idea.

'But I'm not playing second fiddle to no strange female,' she declared firmly as she scoured the spotless house from top to bottom.

Michael too had been abstracted – strangely silent and withdrawn and Sheesha knew he and Beth had disagreed about the honeymoon. He had wanted to carry his bride off to his cottage in Ireland, but she had laughingly said, 'I need sunshine on holiday, darling. I'm like a lazy cat.' Michael loved walking or fishing and hated sunbathing almost as much as he hated cats.

'Perhaps he's getting cold feet about Beth,' thought Sheesha as she opened the curtains, 'they're not very similar people.' Her teeth were chattering so much it was hard to clean them. 'What's the matter with you,' she asked the girl in the mirror, 'why are you so frightened?' Was it having to face Mark? The last time she had seen him was February 14th, the night of the accident. He had been so angry with her then. He had flown over from Ireland especially to give his Aunt Beth away and of course his parents would be there. They had been Sheesha's foster parents until she had practically broken up their marriage and destroyed their household. They would certainly not be pleased to see her.

'Am I scared of going into that church again?' she wondered. 'Those people are so freaked out on God they make me feel embarrassed.' The gong sounded from down below with such terrible force that the door rattled and Sheesha hastily ran downstairs.

'I'll tell Dad I'm just too scared to go,' she thought, but when she reached the dining room, Dolly told her sourly that he had driven off an hour before.

'He's gone to the surgery to see patients,' she growled, 'and said to tell you to be ready by 12.30 sharp.'

'Thanks Dolly,' muttered Sheesha. 'Sorry, I can't manage any breakfast this morning, I feel sick.' Dolly's reply was too fruity to write down and Sheesha decided it would be far safer to be out for a while. 'I'll go to Pippa's house and find out if she's ill,' she decided as the warm sunshine lifted her spirits. She had never been to Pippa's house before, but she knew just where it was. As she walked across the common she realized she knew little about her new friend, except that she had lived with her mother ever since her father had walked out on them a year ago. It was a pretty little Georgian cottage, and rows of daffodils positively beamed at her from the garden. 'How silly to get into such a state over nothing,' she told herself as she rang the bell. 'Premonitions of disaster and all that kind of thing are all in the past.' As she stood on the doorstep a huge removal van drew up at the garden gate and at the same minute the cottage door opened and an older version of Pippa appeared wearing jeans and a worried expression.

Four large men in green aprons converged on the cottage, rolling their sleeves up their tattooed arms. 'Perhaps my premonition of disaster had not been so wrong after all,' she thought as she tried to get out of everyone's way and succeeded only in banging her head on the low beam above the doorway.

'Do start wherever you like,' said Pippa's mother. 'Are you with the removal men, dear?' she added. All Sheesha could see were stars and she sat down heavily on the bottom step of the rickety stairs.

'I came to see Pippa,' she gasped weakly.

'Oh, but she's not here.' The reply seemed to come from a thousand miles away. 'I'm moving in with my boyfriend, so she's decided to go and live with her father. It's all this religious nonsense she's got caught up in since she started to go to that modern church. We had a blazing row on Monday and she packed her bags and went.'

'You mean she's never coming back to school?' said Sheesha, struggling to comprehend the horror of the situation.

'Well, it's time her father took a turn having her, and she'll be going to an excellent school in Scotland. I must look after myself, and it's hard making a new relationship with a teenage girl tagging along behind you. Now if you don't mind you are rather in the way.'

Sheesha staggered away from the little cottage while a deep sympathy for Pippa argued with a feeling of outrage at her mother's callous behaviour. She was halfway across the common before the nasty thought struck her. Maybe her father and Beth would also find it hard to make a new relationship with a teenage girl tagging along behind them. The muddy path under her feet felt suddenly very slippery.

'No wonder she loved Great Aunt Janice so much if she had parents like that,' thought Sheesha. 'I'll go and see her, perhaps she'll have Pippa's address.'

As she slithered over the Common the need for a friend became of paramount importance to her. 'It doesn't matter even if the old girl is ninety,' she told herself, 'she understands me – that's all that counts.'

There sat the little old missionary, swaddled warmly in rugs and shawls as the spring sunshine slanted in on her through the arched doors of the porch.

But something was wrong. 'Don't be silly,' Sheesha told herself firmly. 'Old ladies always look like that when they are asleep.' She put out her hand and laid it gently on the old lady's shoulder, then suddenly she recoiled in horror.

Sheesha fully expected to spend the rest of her life coping with death, but seeing it for the first time was a terrible shock. In a blind panic she turned and ran down the path between the sinister graves. But before she reached the gate she had forced herself to stop. She must be professional like her father would be. She felt for the pulse in her old friend's icy hand, but she knew without a doubt that she would never find one. Two large tears splashed down on the old lady's Bible that still lay open on her lap. 'Oh God, she and Pippa were helping me to find you, why did you take them both away?' she complained.

Wearily she dragged herself towards the phone box on the corner, and then realized that her father's surgery was very near, and he might still be there. Suddenly she longed for him desperately and she began to run as if it were possible to leave far behind her the panic, loneliness and doubt.

Michael was just leaving his consulting room when she pushed open the surgery door.

'Someone's dead in the church,' she gasped and burst into a flood of tears.

Two months before she would have loathed him to touch as much as her hand, but when she felt his arms round her she thought it was the loveliest feeling she had ever known. No one, male or female, had ever loved her enough to hold her in their arms since he had last done it fourteen years before, and suddenly she did not want him ever to let her go. 'This is what it's like to have a father,' she thought, and instantly she recognized the source of her feeling of panic this morning. She had come to love this man so much she did not want to share him with Beth. On the surface she had been looking forward to having a mother, but underneath she resented Beth's intrusion.

'You mustn't get so upset,' said Michael gently, 'you have to learn to take death in your stride in our profession.'

'But she was my friend,' said Sheesha pathetically.

'Well, in that case,' he said gently letting her go, 'it will hurt. Get an ambulance up to the church for us,' he called to his bewildered looking receptionist, and taking Sheesha firmly by the arm, led her back up the road.

A small crowd of sherbet-hungry children had gathered round the old lady when they returned.

'She's only having a nap,' said Michael kindly, 'perhaps you'd better run on home now.' But they looked slightly reluctant, their routine badly upset.

'Here,' said Sheesha, opening the old lady's handbag, and she tossed them the whole bag of sticky sweets. Gleefully they ran away, hardly able to believe their good luck, the last of a long line of children the old doctor had made happy.

Michael took out a wad of death certificates from his pocket and as he began to write, Sheesha looked down at the old missionary. How could she possibly go to a silly giggly wedding when she had received two such heavy blows. It crossed her mind almost as if the old lady had spoken that God would give her power if she asked for it, but she pushed the thought away. She just did not want to go and have people think how fat or how tall or how wicked she was. She didn't want to see Beth squeezed into her wedding dress and looking so happy either. She just wouldn't go.

'That ambulance is taking its time,' remarked her father uneasily. 'We're due at the church in half an hour and we're not even changed.'

Forty minutes later he was hurtling down the stairs, calling, 'Sheesha, let's go love, come on quickly.'

There was no response. The house was silent. Even Dolly, clad in an orange coat of vast dimensions, had left already. Sheesha was not in her room, nor in the lounge, and the best man was hooting his car horn from the drive outside.

'She must have walked,' he thought, and dashed away without her. When the car had gone Sheesha crawled out of the wardrobe and made herself a solitary coffee.

'No one will miss me,' she thought bitterly, 'they'll all be far too busy enjoying themselves.'

Two hours later she was sitting huddled on the sofa in the lounge, when suddenly she heard the key turn in the front door. 'They'll be arriving at the reception in the Fleetbridge Hotel,' she thought, looking at her watch. 'They can't be back yet.' But she dived to the floor behind a large armchair just for safety. It was Mark who entered the lounge. He had borrowed the door key from Michael after the service and had come looking for her. More than a year of patrolling the streets of Belfast had acquired for him the sense of knowing when he was being watched and stealthily he crept across the lounge towards her hiding place.

'Got you!' he shouted, pouncing on her, and pulling her up into his arms. Anger like molten lava swept through Sheesha as she struggled to extract herself. This was typical of Mark. He thought every girl he knew had nothing better to do than fall in love with him.

'My!' he said, stepping back and gazing at her appreciatively. 'You have changed, when I last saw you, you were as thin as a blackbird with its feathers plucked, now you're . . . well . . . something again! Look, I'm sorry for all the things I said that night after the accident, can't we be friends? Your Pop told me you were upset about some old biddy snuffing it this morning, so I came to cheer you up.'

His insufferable way of cheering a girl up was to take her into his arms again and plant a noisy kiss on her lips. All her feminist feelings exploded and she kicked him hard. It was the second time in one morning that she had been embraced by a man, but this time the feeling was far from pleasant.

'Men like you degrade women!' she spluttered.

'But I like you, I find you very attractive,' complained

Mark as he hopped about on his good leg and rubbed the other ruefully.

'You say that to every woman you meet under the age of seventy,' she retorted scornfully.

'You always do this to me,' protested Mark. 'Can't you see you only switch me on when you keep pushing me off. Don't you want to have a nice handsome boyfriend?'

'No,' said Sheesha coldly, 'I don't have time for that kind of thing in my life. I'm going to be a missionary doctor.'

'Well, I can't think what the local lads are doing letting an attractive girl like you slip through their fingers.'

'Could he never be serious?' she fumed.

'Come back to the reception,' he coaxed, 'I'm making a brilliantly funny speech. Been practicing it for days. I'll take you out this evening if you like.'

'I don't like!' she snapped. 'I never go out with boys and I never shall, so go and make your silly speech and leave me in peace.'

'One day you *will* fall in love,' he said, suddenly serious at last, 'and when you do I hope for your sake he loves you back.'

Mark's words came back to Sheesha with sickening clarity a year later, but as she heard him slam the front door, she vowed yet again that she would never allow herself to be enslaved by any man, however goodlooking.

Chapter Four

'What a revoltingly bad way to teach!' thought Sheesha as she sat at the back of the history lesson. Sister Barbara's uninspiring voice droned on as she dictated her usual wad of notes. Sheesha hated history anyway, and they had covered Disraeli in depth a year before at Gravely, so she let her mind wander and gazed about the room. There was an empty desk where Pippa used to sit only a couple of weeks before. 'Why do I feel I need a friend anyway?' wondered Sheesha. 'Can't I just be me, complete in myself, my own person?' Suddenly her eyes encountered Amy's and she hastily turned away to avoid the nasty mocking expression that she sent in Sheesha's direction. 'I shouldn't be affected by insignificant people like that!' she told herself, but all the same she knew that she was. 'Everyone would like me if I looked nice,' she thought as her eyes arrived at Carolyn. 'If only I looked like her.' Carolyn was perfection in miniature, as she sat across the gangway with her immaculate head bent over her book, taking down notes in her neat handwriting. A tiny china doll whose hair was never ruffled by the wind, whose skin never produced spots and whose nails never broke.

Sheesha had been watching her from a distance all the week as the desperate need for a friend mounted within her. She knew that Carolyn lived practically next door in one of the other beautiful houses that ringed the Common. She was the only child of wealthy parents, 'and

I bet they spoil her rotten,' growled Sheesha. 'She wouldn't want to know someone like me.'

'Meggan Davidson!' the icy voice crashed into her thoughts and made her jump. 'You've failed to write down a single note all through this lesson.'

'I don't need to, Sister Barbara,' explained Sheesha. 'I never forget a thing I hear or read so it's a waste of time to take notes.'

'Insolent, arrogant girl!' exclaimed Sister Barbara furiously.

'No I'm not,' replied Sheesha calmly, 'that's just the way my brain works.'

'If you're so clever, then you will write me a four thousand word essay on Disraeli before the end of the week,' spat the history teacher venomously.

'Certainly,' countered Sheesha sweetly. 'But I shall find it hard to confine myself to only four thousand words.' As the class tittered appreciatively, she knew she had won this time, but the look on Sister Barbara's face spelt trouble for her for the future. She was a dangerous enemy to have made, and Sheesha lived to regret her cheap victory.

'Can you really remember everything without making notes?' The bell had gone at last and it was actually Carolyn who had spoken.

'Yes,' replied Sheesha awkwardly, 'I've always been like that.'

'You're a freak!' sneered Amy. 'You're not normal.'

The class clattered away towards the loos where Sheesha knew they would make up ready to face the boys from the Grammar School down the road. 'Brainless hens,' she thought bitterly. This dreadful isolation was the price that all gifted children have to pay for their intelligence. 'They'll all go home now and regurgitate their notes into neat little essays and then think they know all there is to know about Disraeli, and that stupid nun is no better than the rest of them. I'll zap her with the most exhaustive essay I've ever written, even if I have to go without sleep.'

'Well, tonight's the night!' she thought as she walked home across the Common. 'I've always wanted a Mum and a Dad like everyone else, and by tonight I'll have just that.' It had been a strange week since the wedding, all alone in the house except for Dolly, and stuck in a strange kind of a vacuum. She felt she had lost her father, and Beth had not become her mother yet – perhaps she never would. 'I mustn't spoil it all by thinking about that!' she said out loud to a gorse bush. 'Beth isn't going to ruin things, tonight we'll be a real proper cosy family sitting by the fire, and I'll be just the same as Carolyn – two parents with nothing to do but dote on me. Everything's going to be lovely from today on. Even if I don't have a friend at school at least I'll have a mother at home who loves me.'

'This is what it feels like to be a junkie!' thought Sheesha as she gazed down at the pile of biscuits and sweets that littered her bed. Something inside her would compel her to gorge them all that night, gobbling them down without waiting to chew or taste them. Yet she knew she would hate herself in the morning, and panic about her increasing weight. She knew that food binges like this were all part of her recovery from anorexia, but she hated to be controlled by this irresistable compulsion to eat. Everything had gone so terribly wrong that evening, just when she imagined it was going to be so perfect. Food seemed to be the only way to comfort herself, so she had dashed along to the little shop on the corner that stayed open all evening. Her purse was empty now, but her stomach would soon be full. She lay down curling herself round her 'fix' and bit viciously into a bar of chocolate.

Ghastly! ghastly! ghastly! That's what it had been right

from the start of the evening. Dolly had cooked them a welcome home meal using all her culinary skill and the best silver and glass, but the plane from Tenerife had been delayed and her cheese sauce was ruined. She was in such a vile mood when the honeymoon couple finally drove up to the front door that she would not even say hello, but simply beat the bronze gong with even more force than usual.

'I must have a shower before we eat,' laughed Beth, 'I won't be a moment.' But she was nearly an hour, and Dolly was like an enraged Spanish bull by the time she banged the gong for the second time. She was leaving in the morning, but she had wanted this meal to be the climax of her career. Sheesha had thrown down her book on Disraeli at the sound of the thundering gong and hurried downstairs full of good intentions. 'I'll be the sweetest daughter in the world,' she told herself confidently. 'This is going to be the loveliest evening of my life.' But as soon as she walked into the dining room, irritation hit her smack in the face. Beth was sitting in *her* place and she and Michael were laughing at a secret joke they didn't seem to want to share.

'You never came to the wedding,' began Beth in her usual tactless way, 'and there was me longing to show off my new daughter to all my relations.' She was smiling in a way that showed she did not really mind, but Sheesha felt cross that she did not seem to understand how devastating it had been to lose two friends within ten minutes. 'She'll never understand about things that really matter,' Sheesha realized suddenly. 'She's like Winnie the Pooh, a bear of little brain.'

There would be no more reading books at mealtimes now. Beth thought it was unsociable to read in public, but actually she never read in private either. Michael did not seem to be missing his book that evening, however, for they were both full of their holiday and talked about it incessantly.

As the meal progressed Sheesha began to feel more and more in their way. 'They don't really want me now,' she thought bitterly. 'Two's company, three's none and I'm always going to be number three.' What was it Pippa's mother had said about a teenage daughter tagging along?

Beth did her best to bring Sheesha into the conversation, but her loud laughter and constant chatter began to grate on Sheesha's nerves. 'I wanted a mother who was beautiful, elegant, dignified and intelligent,' she thought. 'However did Dad come to marry this untidy idiot?'

'You're putting on weight, my girl,' giggled Beth as they started on Dolly's famous apple pie. 'We'll have to get you some new clothes.' She meant it as a compliment, for Sheesha was certainly beginning to look very attractive, but she could not have said anything more irritating to someone who was sensitive about their size to the point of obsession.

'You're a fine one to talk,' snapped Sheesha and then wished she could swallow her words with the pie, as she saw the hurt look of surprise that crossed her father's face.

The uncomfortable silence that settled over the room was broken by Dolly thumping into the room and demanding fiercely, 'Will you be wanting cheese *as well*?' If she had stirred her foul mood into the sauce she would certainly have poisoned them all with it!

'We couldn't eat another thing, Dolly,' laughed the Doctor. 'You've surpassed yourself.'

'Then I'll take coffee in next door,' she growled and stalked away to relieve her angry feelings by banging the saucepans viciously together in the sink.

'Oh my!' giggled Beth. 'Thank goodness she's going, we'd never cope with her.'

60

'She's only being like that because she feels pushed out and not wanted,' blurted Sheesha, and added under her breath, 'I know how she feels.'

Here they were at last, the idyllic family scene, sitting round the fire, just as Sheesha had pictured them, but it was not working. She had brought down a couple of books on Disraeli, but how can you read when someone constantly addresses futile remarks to you? There was no more Debussy either, Beth didn't like classical music.

'Let's put the telly on,' suggested Beth brightly, 'there's quite a good quiz programme on tonight.'

'I'm going up,' said Sheesha in disgust, 'I've got work to do.' All her fairy tale castles had fallen down round her ears. It was shock and disillusionment that caused her to turn for comfort to food as she had crept out of the front door like an addict in search of heroin.

'What a let down!' she thought as she lay on her bed and bit into yet another biscuit. 'At least I've still got my privacy up here in my room.' But to her horror at that moment someone tapped on her door.

'This is too much,' she thought angrily as she swept her food store under the pillow. 'Is she even going to follow me up here?' But it was her father who walked in, ignoring the chocolate smudges on her cheeks. He sat down beside her, and like the busy GP that he was he came straight to the point.

'You weren't happy at dinner?'

'I'm not used to having a mother,' growled Sheesha, 'I don't know what to do with one.'

'Well, Beth's not used to having a daughter, and I'm afraid you upset her a bit.'

'I upset *her*!' snarled Sheesha. Wearily Michael closed his eyes. He had left Beth crying in the lounge, Dolly crying in the kitchen and now Sheesha was glaring at him up here. What had happened to his peaceful ordered life?

Whatever had he done? Yet it *was* done, he told himself firmly, and leaning forward he took her hand gently in his.

'We must all work together to make this family business a success,' he said. 'You do want it to work, don't you?' Sheesha looked away quickly so that he could not see her eyes. If only she could tell him just *how much* she wanted it to work.

'You don't want me now you've got each other,' she said tentatively and then held her breath in suspense waiting for his reply. But he never had time to make one, for at that untimely moment Beth burst into the room.

'I've been thinking,' she said. 'Let's all ask God to make us a proper family.' She stood beaming hopefully at them while a feeling of suffocating panic seized Sheesha, and she leapt off the bed scattering biscuit crumbs over the luxurious carpet.

'What a typically superficial suggestion,' she snarled as she ran from the room and out into the dying evening.

'She has to bring God into everything,' she fumed as she made for the common, her heartbeat reacting violently to its overload of adrenaline.

It was a wonderful warm evening and the houses round the common looked like enchanted palaces as they poured light out into the shadows from their uncurtained windows.

'That one must be Carolyn's,' thought Sheesha. 'I wonder what real families do when they are relaxing?' The sudden urge to look in through their elegant windows was irresistable, and Sheesha walked towards the low wall that separated their gardens from the common.

The melancholy peace of the evening was shattered as the side door of Carolyn's house was opened with a crash, and Carolyn herself catapulted out into the dusk, her hair untidy and her makeup smudged by tears. They were face to face with each other over the garden wall before Carolyn even saw Sheesha.

'Whatever's the matter?' asked Sheesha.

'Parents!' answered Carolyn bitterly.

'Well that's my problem too,' said Sheesha softly, 'but I always thought you had life sewn up.'

'So did I,' answered Carolyn as the tears and mascara trickled down her face. 'But recently they keep having these terrible rows. They think I can't hear, but I have to listen, I'm almost scared not to. I think Dad's got someone else. Why can't they just grow up! Coping with parents is a nightmare.'

'Well I haven't had a lot of experience,' put in Sheesha grimly, 'but I'm beginning to think you're right.'

'I can't go back in until things have settled down,' said Carolyn miserably.

'Neither can I,' added Sheesha, 'so let's go into town and get a coffee at MacDonalds.'

They were inside the door before they both realised they had come out without any money, and suddenly they were laughing. 'We'd better go and sit in the bus shelter,' giggled Carolyn. 'If we hang round here we'll get picked up.'

'You might,' replied Sheesha, 'but it would take a brave man to pick me up, I can tell you.'

'Oh, you're not that bad looking,' said Carolyn kindly. Sheesha had not meant it quite like that but it was hardly the time to expound her feminist theories.

'We both ought to be doing that Disraeli essay,' sighed Carolyn, 'and you've got four thousand words to do. I wish you'd help me with mine.'

That was the beginning. The relationship was hardly a friendship, but Carolyn was someone to go around with, sit next to in the common room and walk home with at the end of the day. Carolyn's admiration was a balm to Sheesha's damaged self image, even if she did struggle not to fall asleep with boredom in her company.

The letter was lying on the table in the hall when Sheesha got in from school the following day. The writing on the envelope looked like the work of a demented spider and the postmark said Edinburgh. Letters were such a rare occurrence for Sheesha that she had to sit down with shock before she opened it.

Dear Meggan,

Did you think I'd forgotten you? Sorry, but I've been so busy settling into a new school and getting to know Dad all over again and his new girl friend that I haven't had a minute to write.

I was so sad to leave without saying goodbye, but I just had to get away from Mum before I killed her! You'll think I'm mad writing all the way from Scotland to say this, but I feel I must. I just couldn't have lived through these last two weeks without God to help me. I know Dad doesn't really want me up here, and I know Mum wanted to get rid of me too, and I feel totally unwanted and unloved by them, but God's felt so close it is as if He is saying 'It's alright, whatever happens, I'll always love you and I'll never push you off.' I don't suppose you'll ever feel no one wants you – not with a Dad like yours and I've always liked Beth so much when I've talked to her at church, but I just wanted you to know that I'm alright. Did you know Aunt Janice died? I cried for ages when I heard. I know we'll meet again one day, perhaps as undergrads in Oxford?

Much love
Pippa

Sheesha carried the letter upstairs and pinned it above her desk, next to the one that Manda had scrawled for her. Pippa and Manda side by side, Carolyn looked a very poor substitute. But friends who only communicate on paper are not much use against the Amy's of this world. Slowly she picked up the silver cross her father had given her on 'the first day of the rest of her life,' and stood looking down at it. 'Pippa and Manda would both be glad if I put it on, and let God be my boss, but I'm not ready to be hassled by any boss just yet,' she thought. 'I'll show them both that it's possible to cope with parents without God's power,' and she laid the cross and chain back down in its cotton wool bed.

Chapter Five

It was half-term week just before the exams were due to begin and Sheesha had been looking forward to burying herself in the peace of her bedroom in order to put the final touches to her revision. Pre-exam tension had reached terrifying proportions at school and nuns did not seem to be any less prone to it than ordinary teachers would be. As the week went by, however, Sheesha began to wish heartily that she was back in school. It was a large house, but Beth's personality was even larger. The jingly Christian music that she called praise penetrated to every corner of the house, and the sound of her cheerful and lengthy telephone conversations forced its way up through the bedroom floorboards. She was trying desperately hard to be friendly, which caused her to stick her head round Sheesha's door every time she had become engrossed in her work and say, 'I'm just making a coffee, are you coming down?' Sheesha tried very hard to respond, and time after time she closed her books and sat in the cluttered kitchen drinking yet another mug of coffee, but inside she was thinking, 'Doesn't she know what it's like to face ten subjects and to want to get 'A' grades in all of them? I feel as if I've swallowed a bomb and it's only a matter of time before it goes off.' She managed to prevent the bomb from exploding until Friday, but the crater it caused then was massive.

Sheesha had been grappling most of the morning with

history yet again, and all those 19th Century prime ministers were giving her a headache. 'I'll sneak down and get an aspirin,' she thought. 'It's quiet down there for once. She must have gone to the shops.' It was unfortunate that Beth had left the vacuum cleaner on the landing, and even more unfortunate that Sheesha fell over the flex, but worse of all that she crashed heavily backwards right into a tray of dead coffee mugs. A painful experience at the best of times, but infuriating on top of all those dull Parliamentary reforms. 'I wouldn't mind so much,' muttered Sheesha, 'if she ever used the wretched hoover to clean with, but she just leaves it around to deceive people into thinking she does.' The house had gone to pot in the month since Dolly left. Beth believed in the maxim, 'There's a place for everything, but it's much more fun if you keep things somewhere else', and untidiness made Sheesha feel like a hedgehog wearing its prickles inside out.

'Whatever's happened?' demanded Beth rushing out of the spare room where she had been planning a nursery. 'Oh, you've broken four mugs, and they were wedding presents.' It was not really that she was unfeeling, but after a week of trying to make a relationship with Sheesha, even her patience was cracking.

'I couldn't help it,' stormed Sheesha, 'you can't go anywhere in this house these days without falling over dirty crockery.'

'Well, if you gave me a hand with the washing-up sometimes it might help! You treat this place like a hotel!'

'You just don't understand, do you!' yelled Sheesha as the sickly cliché caused the bomb inside her to ignite. 'I've got work to do, I'm not your unpaid slave!'

'Unpaid!' shouted Beth. 'When Michael gives you all that pocket money each week.'

'That's nothing to what other girls at school get!'

snarled Sheesha. 'And anyway he owes it to me, after all I've been through. If you can't cope with the housework, why did you drive Dolly away?'

'Let me tell you my girl . . .' stormed Beth, but Sheesha was past being told anything by this time. 'I'm not *your* girl,' she hissed. 'I never was and I never will be.' And picking up a broken mug from the tray she threw it at Beth with quite remarkable force.

The memory of Beth's astonished expression lived with Sheesha for days. She did not speak – she just stood and let the blood from a jagged cut on her forehead trickle down her face. Suddenly terrified of her own anger, Sheesha flew into the bedroom and turned the key in the lock. As she heard Beth retreating downstairs a terrible feeling of remorse engulfed her. 'Why oh why do I always blow it?' she thought and flung herself down on her satin bedspread and writhed about like a mortally wounded serpent. That cut was deep. It would need stitches. Everyone Beth met for the next few weeks would say, 'How did you do that?' and she would tell them. Then what would everyone think? What would her father say?

The medic who was a continual part of Sheesha's being suddenly asserted itself and she sat upright like a jerky puppet. Suppose Beth had fainted, or was suffering from concussion, she was all alone down there, and very quiet. Guiltily Sheesha ran down the stairs and peered into the kitchen. Beth was sitting at the table holding damp cotton wool to her forehead, and she certainly looked a nasty shade of green.

'Are you alright?' asked Sheesha in a small voice. The very last thing that Sheesha expected to happen was that Beth should laugh, but this is just what she did.

'What a couple of fools we were, yelling at each other like that,' she giggled. 'If you hadn't have thrown that mug at me, I would have chucked it at you! It's not so easy being a family as it looks is it?'

'Will you let me see that cut?' asked Sheesha woodenly. 'It's deep,' she said when Beth removed the cotton wool. 'You'll need stitches. Shall I ring Dad?'

'Goodness no!' laughed Beth, 'He'd fuss like an old hen. Ring for a taxi and we'll go to the hospital. Will you come with me?'

'They'll probably call the police and arrest me for assault,' said Sheesha miserably.

'No they won't; pass me that rolling pin.' Completely bewildered, Sheesha watched her new mother break the kitchen window and then poke her bleeding head through the hole in the glass. 'I'm not going to tell anyone any lies now when I say I put my head through the kitchen window,' she laughed.

'You mean you're not going to tell on me, not even to Dad,' faltered Sheesha.

'Especially not Dad,' said Beth firmly. 'We're going to make a success of this mother and daughter business if it kills us.'

'You look as if it nearly did,' said Sheesha and found herself actually laughing too.

Nothing that Sheesha tried to swallow that morning seemed to want to go down her throat. This was the day her exams began and her stomach felt as if she had eaten all her textbooks and a few pens and compasses for 'afters'.

'I'm going to do better than any other girl ever has at the Sacred Heart,' she told herself firmly as she hugged her mug of black coffee. Breakfast was a very different affair since Dolly left. No longer did they sit in state in the dining room eating boiled eggs from silver cups and thin toast with the crusts cut off. They just rustled round in the untidy cupboard like mice looking for something edible and then ate it standing up or perched at the kitchen table. Dolly would have had apoplexy if she had seen them.

Michael was reading the paper while he fought with the bad-tempered toaster and Beth sat hunched in her dressing gown, her hair standing up like a rough coated guinea pig. 'She looks terrible in the mornings,' thought Sheesha, 'and that cut on her forehead certainly hasn't improved her looks.'

'This toaster will be the death of me!' growled Michael, as two pieces of burnt bread leapt high in the air and then fell onto the dirty floor.

'Proper parents would wish me luck, and make a fuss of me,' thought Sheesha. 'They're so preoccupied I don't suppose they even realize how important today is.' Sheesha was jolted from her self-pity by the extraordinary behaviour of her stepmother. Beth suddenly leapt from the table and dashed towards the downstairs toilet, her chair crashing to the floor in her wake. Michael and Sheesha both politely pretended they could not hear her retching violently.

'Must have caught a bug or something,' said Sheesha to cover their embarrassment. 'Hope I don't catch it during my exams.'

'I don't think it's a bug,' said Michael quietly, while a curious expression flitted across his face. When Beth came bouncing back into the room Sheesha was bewildered to see that her face was beaming, even though it was as green as a frog. 'She looks happier than she did in her wedding photos,' thought Sheesha.

'That's three mornings running,' breathed Beth ecstatically, 'and I can't even face coffee.' Michael leapt across the room tossing the burnt toast in the air, and whooping like a school boy.

'That is wonderful!' he exclaimed as he helped Beth back to her chair.

It was a hot morning, but suddenly Sheesha felt intensely cold as she looked at their happy faces and remembered the medical books she had read in her father's study. What a fool she had been never to realize that a thing like this could happen, even to people as old as this. Of course they would have a baby of their own. That explained the odd telephone conversation she had overheard the day before. Beth had said, 'I hope it's a boy, men always want a son.' Of course it would be a son, she could picture him already, lean and suntanned, good at sport and brilliant at work. He would probably become a professor of medicine while she was stuck as a GP. 'Men always want a son.' The statement went on echoing in her mind like a funeral bell. Once Michael had a boy of his own he wouldn't want a second-hand, shop-soiled daughter any more, and all Beth's love and attention would naturally be given to her own child. Silently she left the kitchen, leaving them to gaze ecstatically into each other's eyes. 'I just don't exist for them now,' she thought bitterly, 'just when I thought we were beginning to get on alright.'

The hall at school was hot and stuffy, even at 9.30 in the morning. The dark oak panels were oppressive, and flies buzzed about the cobwebs that decorated the stained glass windows. Sheesha slid rather shakily into the desk that was just one of the many standing in long rows. Sister Barbara on the dais at the front looked at her watch and cleared her throat officially. Sheesha groped for her pencil case, trying to find her pen, but her fingers did not work, they felt numb and dead, just like she felt inside. How could she possibly write a history paper after a blow like this. 'I'll just have to tell them I'm ill,' she thought.

'You may open your papers now, and begin,' said the cold voice of the nun and a wave of agitated rustling filled the hall. Sheesha never moved, she just sat gazing blankly in front of her. 'You could run away,' said the old familiar voice in her head, 'after all, they wouldn't care, not now they're going to have their own baby. Just get up and walk out of here, and disappear. It would serve them right.'

The cold hen's claw fingers were on her shoulder as Sister Barbara bent forward to turn her paper over, tapping it with an impatient finger nail. 'You'd like me to fail,' thought Sheesha looking up into the dark shrunken face above her, 'so you could say "I told you so." ' She glanced down idly at the paper and her face twisted into a grim smile as she caught sight of the first question. 'How influential was Disraeli in the passing of the 1867 Parliamentary Reform Bill?' 'That's a cinch for me,' she thought, picking up her pen. Suddenly there was an ominous slithering thump from the other side of the aisle and Sheesha looked up to see Carolyn sinking to the floor in a faint. Sheesha knew how terrified Carolyn had been about these exams. Obviously the strain was too much. She lay between the rows of desks like a fragile broken doll. 'Beth called *me* a broken doll once,' thought Sheesha as she watched two nuns scoop her up and carry her away to the Medical Room. 'How dare she call me that! I'll show them I'm not made like the Carolyns of this world!' She squared her shoulders and turned to Disraeli with a sudden angry vigour. Perhaps they won't have a boy, or maybe it'll be brainless like its mother. Perhaps it will even die at birth. With this comforting thought in the back of her mind she proceeded to write a completely brilliant history paper, and walked out of the hall three hours later feeling refreshed and peaceful.

'I came to see how Carolyn is,' said Sheesha, as the elegantly panelled door swung slowly open. She was on her way home from school when an impluse had decided her to turn into the well kept drive. After all, she had no particular desire to get back to her own home today.

'You're Doctor Davidson's daughter, aren't you?' said Carolyn's mother. Everything about her clothes, hair and makeup was perfect but Sheesha had always been able to see right through people and as she looked down at Mrs Ridgeway she knew something was badly wrong with her. 'Come in, perhaps you can cheer her up,' she said and standing back she motioned Sheesha towards the elegant drawing room. Carolyn was lying on a chaise-longue propped up by mounds of tasteful patchwork cushions and she looked like something out of a Jane Austen book. She did not speak however, and her face seemed frozen stiff while her delicate fingers twitched in an oddly unnatural way.

'It's not such a tragedy,' smiled Sheesha, 'you always do well in course work. Anyone might be taken ill, they'll let you sit it again.'

'It's not that,' said Carolyn in a choked unsteady voice. 'Who cares about a silly exam?'

'What's the matter, then?' asked Sheesha, suddenly remembering her mother's face in the hall.

'Promise you won't tell anyone at school,' pleaded Carolyn. 'Daddy's gone, we discovered his note this morning.'

'That's rather a mean way of wishing you luck with your exams,' said Sheesha sarcastically. 'You'd think he might have waited until after you'd done them. My parents sprung a mean one on me this morning, it almost finished my chances too.' Carolyn wasn't listening, she just sat staring at the antique clock on the mantelpiece.

'I just can't face having to live with Mum,' she said distantly. 'I've always got on best with my Dad.'

'Then why don't you go and live with him, like Pippa did,' suggested Sheesha.

'He's gone off with his secretary,' answered Carolyn bitterly. 'She's not much older than I am and stepmothers never want teenagers hanging around, do they?' Sheesha felt she was watching a film for a second time through, and the repetition sickened her.

'No I suppose they don't,' she said heavily, 'especially when they are pregnant.'

'How do you know she's pregnant?' asked Carolyn sharply.

'Oh, I don't know about yours, but mine is, that's why she won't want to bother with me now. Why don't you get on with your mother? She looks so like you.'

'I know,' growled Carolyn, 'that's what I hate about her most. I think I'll just freak out, I won't go back to school any more.'

'What did you want to do when you leave?' asked Sheesha.

'I thought I'd do beauty therapy,' replied Carolyn, 'that's what Mum did.'

'Ugh!' grimaced Sheesha. 'Fancy fiddling around with people's fingernails and pulling out their eyebrows. Why don't you do something worthwhile?'

'I'd quite like to be an air hostess,' said Carolyn hopefully.

'You're being strangled by your female mentality,' said Sheesha loftily. 'What's wrong with engineering?'

Carolyn looked horrified. 'I think I'll just freak out, thanks,' she said.

At that moment Mrs Ridgeway appeared, pushing a trolley neatly laid for afternoon tea. Tiny cucumber sandwiches and dainty little cakes lay on doily covered plates. Sheesha looked at her in amazement. Her life had fallen apart, yet she could still produce a tea like this.

It was quite a rude shock to the system to arrive home a couple of hours later. The kitchen was the kind of rubbish tip that would have made Dolly expire with horror; the breakfast things still littered the table, piles of dirty washing lay waiting to be put into the washing machine, the ironing was stacked in the corner like a mini mountain and bags of deserted shopping littered the floor. Michael stood in the middle of the room looking completely helpless as he clutched a saucepan and a wooden spoon.

'Thank goodness you've come back at last,' he said rather crossly. 'Have you any idea how to cook scrambled eggs?'

'Where's Beth then?' asked Sheesha acidly.

'She's in bed, she's been terribly sick all day.'

'Well, I've got a lot of revision to do for tomorrow. I can't start doing housework.'

'And I've got surgery in half an hour,' snapped Michael, 'and I'm starving.'

'You should have married someone like Carolyn's mother,' snarled Sheesha. 'Some women don't flop into bed at the first sign of difficulty.'

'That's not fair!' shouted her father. 'Look, Beth's nearly forty. You know enough about obstetrics to know that's a very dangerous age to have a first baby. There's going to be a high risk of toxaemia unless she rests a lot. We'll be counting on you to help us through.'

'So that's all I'm good for now, is it,' yelled Sheesha. 'You just want me for what you can get out of me – work! Why don't you change my name from Sheesha to Cinderella? You don't even care enough about me to ask how my history went – get your own scrambled eggs.' And she ran out of the room.

Chapter Six

Life went on. 'It always does,' thought Sheesha grimly. The only good thing about Beth's baby was that it kept her in bed or being sick in the loo, so Dolly came back for a few hours each morning, and when she had finished grumbling about the mess, she soon had it cleared. The exams went like magic. Every paper seemed to have been written just for her, and when she looked at Carolyn and Amy staggering round school like zombies she began to feel that being gifted was worth all the hassle after all. At home she kept to her room like a monk to his cell, but Michael was so busy and Beth so sick that neither of them seemed to notice. Carolyn went off to stay with her aunt in Scotland as soon as the exams were over, and suddenly it was the end of term and Manda's second letter arrived.

Dear Sheesha,

I hope you're impressed with the writing. I am out of traction and it's so much easier to write sitting up in my wheelchair. I am fine from the waist up, but not so good lower down! Never mind, the 'physios' are working on that like mad.

You said in your last letter that you were beginning to live happily ever after. You will never know how that has helped me to cope with life here. It all seems worthwhile. I've got to go now for hydrotherapy,

Much love,
                    Your friend Manda.

The letter upset Sheesha so much she went straight into a
food binge spiral, and ten minutes later she was sitting
among the gorse bushes on the common stuffing herself
with a large loaf of white bread, hot from the baker's shop.
'How am I ever going to write back?' she wondered when
she began to feel as sick as Beth. 'She's coping with life
because she thinks I'm happy! What am I going to tell
her?' When she had finished the loaf, plus three
doughnuts and a gingerbread man she staggered home,
and sat down at her desk to write, the reassuring sound of
Dolly hoovering the lounge beneath her being strangely
comforting.

Dear Manda,
        Thanks for writing. Life is MEGGA! The exams
    were a cinch . . .
It was then that her inspiration began to dry up, but she
carried on bravely.

Next month – if Beth is better – we are actually going on
holiday to Dad's cottage in Ireland. I've never been on a
real holiday in my whole life before. It's going to be
great. Dad says it's right in the wilds surrounded by
nothing but moors and peat bogs. I know Beth doesn't
want to go, she likes the sun and lots of shops, but Dad
says he walks miles there and he's going to show me all
his special places.

She did not add that she hated walking and fully expected
to be forced to do all the chores.

Mark is coming up from Belfast for a weekend leave.

She tried hard to say, 'that will be nice', but even as practiced a liar as she was could not go that far. Neither did she add, 'for such a nice person as you are, you certainly have some odd relations!' At last she finished:

It's just the sort of holiday you'd love . . .

She'd written the words before she could stop herself, but did not cross them off, simply added,

Work hard on your physio then you can come with us next year.

Then she stuffed the letter into an envelope and hoped Manda would not read between the lines.

There, above her desk was Pippa's scrawl. She had replied but had never heard from her again. 'Shall I write her a truthful letter, and tell her all the things I couldn't let Manda know about?' she wondered. But then with sudden finality she realised how impossible that would be. Pippa had heard Old Sherbet Lemons say, 'God will give us power to live with irritating people, but sometimes we are just too cross to ask Him for it.' Pippa would simply quote those words back to her, and remind her that God would never stop caring about her, even if her parents did. No, she couldn't write to Pippa unless she was willing to let God help her. So she banged a stamp on to Manda's letter, and bought a huge bar of chocolate on the way to the post box.

'I'm not leaving until the post comes,' said Sheesha, sitting down firmly on the door stop.

'But we'll miss the boat if we don't go now,' said Michael impatiently heaving himself out of the heavily loaded car.

'But the Exam results are sure to come today,' continued Sheesha, 'and I must know how I did.'

'Look, we'll leave a note for Dolly and ask her to send all your letters on,' promised Michael.

'The postman will be here any minute,' retorted Sheesha, and Michael sighed wearily. He felt he had aged considerably over the last six months.

'Look,' he said patiently, 'we're going on holiday together for the first time ever, couldn't we just make a pact to be nice to each other for two weeks?'

'Alright,' agreed Sheesha, 'you start by being nice enough to wait for my results.' Michael turned and began rechecking the contents of the roof rack. For years he'd been setting off for the cottage like this in August, his fishing tackle and climbing boots in the back, and a picnic hamper prepared by Dolly on the seat beside him. Loads of books to read and no one to please but himself, but now . . . He knew Beth didn't want to go. She hated walking almost as much as she hated reading. No electricity, no bath and only a loo in the garden shed. Whatever would she do all day? For years he had dreamt of taking his little Meggan to the cottage, and he'd even been fool enough to imagine her there with him even when he thought she was dead, but would the real Meggan enjoy his secret place? He had enjoyed his orderly life. He had not married because he was lonely, he just felt that he had let himself become cut off from the hassle of ordinary family life, and he'd been right! This time next year they'd have a carry cot and piles of nappies to take as well. Had it all really been worth it?

'Here comes the postman at last,' shouted Sheesha, cutting through his gloomy thoughts just as Beth came out of the house carrying her inevitable knitting.

'They've probably got the results at school,' she said in a disappointed voice as she thumbed through the dull looking letters, none of which were addressed to her. 'Could we ring Sister Gertrude?'

'Not at this time of the morning,' bellowed Michael. 'We're supposed to be going on holiday, remember?'

'I sweated my guts out doing those exams, and you don't even care how I did!' muttered Sheesha flinging herself angrily into the back of the car. Michael locked the front door, which Beth in her usual happy way had left standing wide open, and with another sigh he slammed the car door shut and let the overloaded car trickle out of the drive.

The wind tore off the moors and goaded the rain into a horizontal attack on the thatched roof of the little cottage. Inside, the peat fire hissed in protest and the light of the oil lamps wobbled in the draught. Sheesha sat in the huge armchair, her long spidery legs curled under her and wrote, balancing the writing pad on the arm of the chair – this letter was going to be easy to write because this time she could be really truthful.

Dear Manda,

I thought I'd write and share all this with you, and how you would love it here. I'll bring you to this place if I have to swim the Irish Sea with you in the wheelchair! I don't think I've ever enjoyed anything so very much. You would have been proud of me today. Dad and I must have walked twenty miles at least, I never thought I could walk one! And he showed me all his secret, favourite places. He's brought me some proper walking boots and a cagoule. We are sitting by the fire now, happily exhausted. Beth is knitting a shawl for *THE BABY*, and the pattern is so complicated she's not able to keep talking. Dad's reading and I have to keep pinching myself in case this is only a dream. At home we all tend to go our separate ways a bit, but here you have to be together, because there's only one room downstairs and then you go up a ladder to one big room in the rafters. (There's a little curtained-off bit for me.) I feel I'm getting to know them both much better. Dad is so like me! And he's real fun to be on holiday with.

'Sugar!' exclaimed Beth shattering the peace and the cosy silence. 'I've dropped another stitch. I'm going to make some hot chocolate.' Now she was better she had begun to bounce again like a ball with its puncture mended. Sheesha put down her pen with a sigh of resignation and Michael laid aside his book. Suddenly their eyes met across the fireplace and the look of annoyance faded from their eyes as they smiled at each other in mutual understanding. 'He feels as cross as I do,' thought Sheesha in amazement.

'I'm going down the garden to the loo while the milk boils,' continued Beth as she lit the camping stove and struggled into her boots and waterproofs. Suddenly and unexpectedly she began to giggle. 'If only my staff nurses could see me now,' she said as she fought her way out into the rain.

'That's why I love Beth,' said Michael, almost to himself. 'That laugh.'

'I'm not very good at laughing,' admitted Sheesha. 'I feel things too deeply.'

'You inherited that from me,' said her father. 'I'm sorry. But I think we'd be wrong if we thought Beth didn't feel things deeply. It's just that she's learnt to make laughter her safety valve – she could teach us a lot. She's a very different sort of person to you and me. We'll have to work hard to make her happy.'

'Make *her* happy?' said Sheesha in startled surprise. The idea had never entered her head.

'I think we both only consider how *she* could make *us* happy, and that's been the cause of our trouble.' Their eyes met again, and Sheesha found herself wishing she could stop the video and prevent this moment of intimacy from being carried away from her for ever. Never before had she ever felt this close to another human being. 'We could have been so happy together, just him and me,' thought Sheesha sadly, 'if only he hadn't married this crazy woman. And then he tells me we've got to make her happy!' At that moment Beth bundled herself back into the room, dripping wet and talking loudly, and the barrier went back up between Michael and his daughter.

'If the weather clears tomorrow, I'd like to teach you both to fish,' he said as they drank their hot chocolate.

'Is it a long walk to the river?' asked Beth suspiciously.

'We can take the car at least halfway,' said Michael evasively.

'You two go,' laughed Beth, 'I'm too old to wade about in cold water. I'll stay here and conquer this shawl; I've got the radio for company.'

The rain had stopped next morning and the sun smiled in through the cottage windows. Beth waved them away with their rucksacks full of sandwiches and their rods over their shoulders. It was not until they were out of sight that she allowed the smile to slide from her face and the tears of loneliness to splash down on to her knitting.

The river lay in a deep gorge with high rocky walls towering above its brown peat-stained water.

'We'll walk up this little path for about half a mile,' explained Michael, 'and then the gorge widens out – it's perfect for fishing.'

It was an enchanting place when they finally arrived. Two rivers met leaving a flat little shaley beach overhung by beech trees.

'This,' said Sheesha crouching down on a mossy

boulder, 'is the loveliest bit of all the world.' Her father looked down at her and smiled.

'I've always thought that too,' he said softly.

'Whoever lives in that little cottage is mighty lucky,' commented Sheesha, pointing to a perfect little stone cottage nestling among the rocks.

'No one lives there,' replied her father. 'It must be someone's holiday place, but I've never seen them in it.' Sheesha ran over to take a closer look. She never had been able to resist looking in other people's windows.

'It's lovely inside,' she called, 'all furnished and fitted out.'

'I think someone from the village must come and clean it,' said her father, joining her at the window.

'It's a wonder squatters don't come and live in it,' commented Sheesha, 'they could easily break the window and climb in.'

'This place reminds me of you,' said Michael, pressing his nose against the glass.

'Me? Why?'

'Jesus said that someone who'd had an evil spirit cast out of them was just like a house that's been all cleaned up, and left furnished and empty.'

'How odd,' said Sheesha, 'that's just how I do feel inside – empty.'

'Jesus said people like you are in great danger. Because you *are* empty the evil spirit might come back and get inside again, bringing along his friends to make their home in you.'*

'No they won't!' flashed Sheesha. 'Why should they?'

'Simply because you have left yourself empty. You haven't asked God to come and fill you up with all that is wonderful about Him, His love, peace, happiness, kindness, self control and all that kind of thing.' Sheesha

*The story can be found in Matthew 12:43–45.

stood looking at the little empty cottage for a long time. 'Anger, bitterness and hate,' continued her father, 'they ruled you before – watch they don't climb back in through the windows.'

'Stop preaching,' laughed Sheesha, 'and let's have lunch.'

They never meant to be so late, it was just that time stood still in that lonely gorge.

'It's nearly seven o'clock!' exclaimed Michael guiltily. 'Whatever will Beth say?'

'Plenty, as usual,' sighed Sheesha, and reeled in her line.

As they walked back along the narrow riverside path, both their minds were racing and churning like the turbulent water beside them. Sheesha, carrying the rods over her shoulder, told herself bitterly that she had been too happy that day. 'Soon he'll bring his son here to his private heaven and share it all with him. "Men always want a son." ' Beth's words pounded in her head like a continuous roar of the river. 'Then he won't want me any more.'

Michael, striding along carrying their catch and the rest of the tackle, also felt he had been too happy that day. It was being an increasing delight to find a mirror image of himself in this daughter he thought he had lost. Yet the closer he grew to Sheesha the further he felt from Beth. He really loved Beth, and they would have been so happy together if Sheesha had not exploded into their lives. He was not being fair to Beth to leave her alone every day in a cottage he knew she hated. After all, they had only been married a few months. Yet he knew instinctively that Beth would never enjoy doing the things he liked to do, as Sheesha did. If he was going to make anything of his marriage he must try to meet Beth at least half way, but that would mean soft-pedalling his growing relationship with Sheesha, who he sensed would always try and pull him away from his new wife.

'Oh God,' he prayed, 'this whole situation is too much for me. How can I possibly learn to live with two women at once?'

Suddenly he caught sight of a dipper – a tiny, frail-looking bird flitting from boulder to boulder, low over the surface of the turbulent water. 'If God can make anything as perfect as that tiny creature,' thought Michael, 'He can certainly look after my family.'

'That's funny,' commented Sheesha as they neared their cottage an hour later, 'no smoke coming out of the chimney.' They pushed open the door and both stood still in surprise. There was no fire, no supper and no Beth.

'The car's here,' said Michael, 'she can't have gone anywhere.'

'Perhaps she's in bed,' suggested Sheesha, and ran up the ladder to the loft. There lay Beth huddled in a sleeping bag, her face white and tearstained.

'Dad!' called Sheesha urgently, 'come here quick!' Michael pushed past Sheesha and hurried to the bed.

'Darling, what's happened?' he demanded.

'I think I'm losing the baby,' sobbed Beth. 'I didn't know what to do.'

'Well, of course you did just the right thing lying flat,' said Michael, suddenly the doctor again. 'The journey to hospital over the rough tracks would be disastrous, but forunately I came prepared. Sheesha, get my case from downstairs, and I'll give her an injection at once.'

'Well, that's the end of the holiday,' thought Sheesha bitterly, as she filled a hot water bottle. 'We'll just have to stay in with her now and do all the chores as well, and if that isn't enough, Mark will be here next week. I should have remembered it's dangerous for me to be happy!' Her letter to Manda finished rather abruptly and not quite so sincerely as it had begun.

The sun shone brilliantly all the following week, painting the hills and moors with constantly changing colours.

Michael spent his time sitting with Beth, 'I can't be sure without a scan, but I'm pretty certain the baby's fine,' he said, and his confidence put a smile back on Beth's face.

'They seem more wrapped up in each other than ever now,' thought Sheesha, and once again felt the odd one out, 'and it'll be even worse when the baby's born.' Whenever she could get away from the endless washing up she spent her time tramping alone over the deserted coutryside, listening to the birds and the cry of the sheep.

'If only that baby would die,' she thought viciously, as she struggled up the highest hill in the district.

'That's right,' encouraged the voice in her head. 'If you wish it dead hard enough it will die.'

'That's murder,' argued the other, better side of Sheesha.

'It's not a baby yet, only a three month old foetus,' the voice continued. 'Doctors are killing them every day. You'll have to do it one day yourself.'

Suddenly she stopped and leaned her back against a lump of weather beaten stone. The memory of the lab at Gravely flashed into her mind. A glass bottle on the shelf, with a label that read, 'Three month foetus'. She had stood gazing at the tiny thing, noticing the perfection of its fingers, legs and minute toes. A human being in everything but size. Even with her head full of feminist ideas she had still felt outraged at the whole idea of deliberate abortion. Yet back at the cottage just such a tiny being was fighting for survival.

'I still want it to die,' she shouted to a startled sheep, who watched in amazement as she beat her fists against the rock in a helpless agony of frustration. The intensity of her hatred frightened her. She had not felt like that since she had become Meggan Davidson.

The thought of Mark's arrival was as irritating as a sharp stone in the shoe to Sheesha. 'Can't we ring and tell him Beth's ill,' she protested.

'No, let him come,' laughed Michael. 'It will cheer Beth up to have her favourite nephew around, and I'll be happier knowing you're not out there walking on your own.'

'Mark's not the type for country walks,' retorted Sheesha. 'He likes the bright lights and a pub on every corner.'

But it was not the Mark they knew who crawled out of his ancient car at three o'clock on a Friday afternoon. He looked pale and strained and his eyes were bloodshot with tension. Beth was downstairs for the first time and sitting by the fire, and they plied their visitor with vast amounts of food, which was always the best thing to do for Mark, but he ate mechanically, as if the food had no taste whatever.

'It's a lovely evening,' said Michael, 'why don't you two go for a nice long walk?' They neither of them wanted to go, Sheesha because she was frightened of being alone with Mark, and Mark because he simply wanted to crawl into bed and sleep forever.

'Take him up to the gorge,' said Michael.

'That's our place,' argued Sheesha.

'No it's not,' protested Michael, with a guilty look at Beth, 'it's the local beauty spot.'

'It *is* our place,' fumed Sheesha to herself as they set out, 'it's just the sort of spot where Mark'll start making a pass at me.'

But this was a different Mark who trudged along in silence behind her. 'What's the matter with you?' she demanded when they stopped in the entrance of the gorge for him to light yet another cigarette.

He lifted his dull lifeless eyes to her face, and inhaled the smoke deeply. 'You couldn't possibly understand,' he said bitterly. 'No Fleetbridge kid could possibly understand what it's like in Belfast.'

'I might,' replied Sheesha. 'I've read books.'

'Books,' sneered Mark. 'They'd never tell you how it feels to be constantly hated. You see it in people's eyes – even the kids. Wherever you go, there they stand on the street corners wishing you dead. It gets you down after a bit.'

'Can wanting someone dead actually kill them?' asked Sheesha guiltily.

'Put a gun in those people's hands, and they'd stop wishing us dead and just pull the trigger, so I suppose wishing someone dead is most of the way towards killing them. I guess you think I'm cracking up,' he continued edgily, as he threw his match into the river and watched it bobbing away.

'Are you?' asked Sheesha bluntly.

'It's stupid,' he said with a shudder. 'I even thought I was being followed all the way today. perhaps I am going to pieces. I went to see Manda a couple of weeks ago,' he went on, as they began to walk up the river path. 'She's really got this religion business badly, hasn't she? Are you into it too?'

'No,' said Sheesha firmly, 'I'm my own person.'

'Well, when you look round that hospital, you have to admit she stands out,' said Mark thoughtfully. 'Lots of them there have just gone crackers, can't cope with their lives at all, but she seems to have grown up years. She says God gives her the power to cope.'

'Manda with power!' thought Sheesha in disgust. 'It was always me with the power, and she was the weak one, doing as she was told!'

'She said God would give me power to cope too,' said Mark softly. 'Do you think it's worth asking Him?' But Sheesha never replied because just at that moment they rounded the corner and there was the place where the two rivers met.

'Look!' quavered Sheesha. 'Look at the cottage.' Without waiting for a response from Mark she began to run towards the little place that had seemed so safe and cosy just a few days before. All the windows were smashed and the door stood open, flapping on a broken hinge.

'Look out! Someone might still be in there,' warned Mark, suddenly the wary soldier again.

'Who cares!' said Sheesha, almost sobbing with indignation as she plunged through the battered door. Everything inside was desecrated, the furniture turned over, the contents of drawers thrown on the floor, pictures and curtains slashed with a knife and IRA slogans written over the walls in red paint.

'People shouldn't leave their cottages empty,' said Mark without emotion, 'that's asking for trouble.'

'Dad said this is what could happen to me,' said Sheesha.

'Happen to you?' said Mark blankly.

'I just wanted to keep myself empty and not be pushed about by anything.'

'We all feel like that when we're young,' said Mark, suddenly feeling old at twenty-one, 'but no one *can* stay empty as you call it, not forever. Sooner or later something or someone always comes in and controls us.'

'You're as bad a preacher as Dad,' complained Sheesha.

'Well, if you don't believe me, join the army or fall in love,' said Mark, peering uneasily out of the broken window. 'Come on,' he said tensely. 'Let's get away from here, I can't seem to get it out of my head that someone's watching me.'

It must have been about midnight and they were still sitting round the fire. Mark had eaten what he called a small snack but which was a meal that would have kept most people going for a week. Beth's infectious laughter worked on him like a tranquilliser and now he lay slumped in his chair, relaxing at last and recounting endless army jokes, each one bluer than the last.

Outside the weather had broken and an angry wind was screaming in from the moors, and forcing itself down the old chimney.

'It feels so safe in here,' said Beth happily as her knitting needles clicked. 'I think I'm getting very fond of this old place after all.' During the first lonely week of the holiday she thought she was losing Michael for good, but since the uncertainty over the baby they had been closer than they had ever been before.

Suddenly Sheesha uncurled her long legs and sat up very straight in her chair. On the far side of the fire Mark stiffened too, his sleepy eyes suddenly alert, they had neither of them heard anything, out there in the darkness, but they had both felt instinctively that they were surrounded by danger.

'Someone's out there,' said Sheesha nervously.

'Couldn't possibly be,' laughed her father, 'no one comes within miles of here at night. You must have heard a sheep.'

'It wasn't a sheep,' said Mark, springing to his feet. 'When you have to patrol the streets of Belfast you develop a kind of antenna for danger, and mine is going berserk. I wasn't imagining it, someone really was following me all day.'

'Who would follow you?' said Beth, attempting a half-hearted laugh.

'They're doing this to servicemen on leave at the

moment,' said Mark grimly. 'The safest place to take a holiday is in the barracks these days.'

'They wouldn't track you all the way up here,' said Michael moving towards the window.

'Don't touch that curtain!' ordered Mark urgently. 'They mustn't know we're on to them. I suppose I'll have to tell you this, that ever since that kidnapping affair last year, I've been a marked man. The army discovered a huge store of ammo and guns when they found us, so we haven't been popular with these guys since. One of the other men who was with me in that affair was shot just a few weeks back.'

Beth made a little broken noise in her throat and allowed her precious white knitting to slip onto the floor.

'Where's the telephone?' asked Mark.

'There isn't one,' replied Michael, 'I come here especially to get away from the thing. Look, I think you're imagining all this, you need a long holiday. You're suffering from nervous exhaustion, I can read the signs.'

'What's that?' asked Beth sharply.

'Someone's on the roof over the kitchen,' breathed Sheesha.

'They'll be setting light to the thatch to force us outside,' said Mark flatly.

'Well it'll never catch,' put in Beth hopefully. 'With all that rain last week it must be sodden.'

'Anything'll catch if you use enough petrol,' said Mark, 'and this wind'll help too.'

'This just can't be happening,' exclaimed Michael, as Mark disappeared up the ladder to the loft.

'Smoke's coming through the rafters,' reported Mark. 'I reckon we've got about ten minutes left.'

'My knitting!' exclaimed Beth, 'I'm not leaving that to burn.'

'How futile can you get,' thought Sheesha, but she

picked up the book she was reading and stuffed it into her cagoule pouch all the same.

'Is there another way out of this place?' asked Mark.

'Just the one door, I'm afraid,' replied Michael.

'Will they just be standing out there waiting to pick us off as we walk out?' said Beth in horror.

'It's me they want,' replied Mark gruffly, 'you should be alright.'

'Haven't we got anything we can shoot them with first?' shouted Sheesha in a sudden spurt of anger.

'Well, I naturally didn't bring a rifle on leave with me,' said Mark witheringly.

'Why don't you disguise yourself – put on one of my skirts and a woolly hat?' suggested Beth.

'Dear old Auntie Beth,' said Mark gently hugging her. 'They know I'm in here, they'll shoot you all if they don't see me at once.'

'Well, I don't know what we're doing standing here wasting time,' said Beth with sudden energy. 'We ought to be praying.'

'What if we don't all believe in prayer,' said Mark uncomfortably.

'Who cares as long as it works,' said Sheesha, surprising herself. They knelt down on the rag rug by the fire and joined hands. Sheesha could never afterwards remember what Michael prayed, all she could think of as soon as she closed her eyes was the old lady and her sherbet lemons. The story of the bandits in Tibet came back to her mind. 'God gave us the power, and they dropped their eyes and just walked away.' The words floated back to her, and suddenly she found herself praying silently. 'I'm sorry God, I've let myself stand empty so long, one day I'll do something about that, but in the meantime, please give us your power to get out of here safely.'

Thick choking smoke was beginning to billow down

from the loft, making their eyes water and their throats sore.

'We'll have to get out of here right now,' said Michael tersely, 'there's nothing else we can do.'

'I'll go first then,' said Mark, squaring his shoulders. 'Get your car keys ready, and we'll try and make a dash for it.'

'No,' said Sheesha suddenly. 'You won't go first, why should men always be the little heroes?'

'Because women just aren't cut out for this kind of thing,' replied Mark condescendingly.

'I'd rather be shot than patronised by an arrogant male like you,' snarled Sheesha. 'You think all women are soft.'

'This is hardly the time to discuss the feminist movement,' growled Mark and walked purposely towards the door. But Sheesha was too quick for him, she darted forward and stuck out her large foot. At any other time she would have enjoyed the sight of him falling to the ground, felled by a mere woman, but there was no time for gloating that night, and it scarcely registered with her that Mark had hit his head on the heavy iron doorstop and was lying ominously still.

As soon as she opened the door the wind gushed in, and up the ladder, causing a frightening acceleration of the fire, and flames began to devour their beds and possessions. Sheesha was only dimly aware of Michael and Beth bending over Mark as she stepped out of the door. She braced herself for the sound of gunfire or the sight of masked figures surrounding her, but she encountered nothing but the wind and the empty darkness. By the light of the dancing flames she could see the outline of their two cars parked on the track at the far side of the rough stone wall. Slowly and deliberately she began to walk towards them, fighting back her panic. She had reached the gap in the wall that had once supported a garden gate, when she heard someone cock a rifle deep in the sinister shadows and she froze. The tall figure of a man materialised beside her and she could smell the stale beer on his breath. He was barring her way to the cars and he seemed to have no intention of moving. Remembering Great Aunt Janice she fixed her eyes on the blur that was his face and moved slowly towards him. A surge of anger filled her body. Here he stood, confident behind his gun, swaggering in his self designed uniform. He was nothing but a bully and male. How she hated men! How dare he destroy the place she and her father loved so much?

Behind her she was dimly aware of Michael and Beth dragging the limp body of Mark over the sheep-cropped grass, but her eyes never left the face in front of her.

'Will I give it to 'er, Sean?' came a hoarse voice from the dark side of the wall.

''Tis only a kid,' said the man in her pathway, 'hold your fire a while.'

'You can't shoot us,' she said, trying to imitate the valiant tones of the old missionary doctor. 'We're under the protection of God!' Slowly the man lowered his rifle just as Michael and Beth reached the car, and began heaving and rolling Mark into the back seat, but Sheesha never moved as she concentrated every atom of her energy into the man before her.

'Sheesha, come on!' shouted Michael urgently, but still she did not move.

'Leave the girl, we'll shoot the car,' came the hidden voice and it had a rasp of anger now.

'You will not shoot the car, or anything else,' said Sheesha evenly. 'I told you before. God won't let you.'

Suddenly the headlights of Michael's car flashed full on, and for the first time Sheesha saw the man's face clearly. The image scorched itself into her mind, and she knew with a sickening sensation that she would see it again one day. The car slid slowly up behind her as the man melted away into the gloom.

She fell into the back seat on top of a dazed and groaning Mark and they were bumping away over the track before she allowed herself to take another breath.

'That's just not possible,' gasped Mark when the burning cottage was far behind them. 'Why did they let us get away?'

'I told them they couldn't shoot us, God wouldn't let them,' replied Sheesha simply. 'After all we prayed He'd keep us safe.'

'You just stood there and said that to an IRA man, with his rifle poked up your nose? You're the most amazing girl I've ever met.'

'She certainly was incredibly brave,' said Michael, 'but it was God who really saved our lives.'

'I don't understand about all this religion,' said Mark, 'it's too much for me. You'll have to stop, I'm going to be sick!'

'Concussion,' said Michael and Sheesha in unison, as Mark leapt from the car.

Chapter Seven

It felt strange to be back in her bedroom in Fleetbridge again. The smell of peat, wood smoke and heather were replaced by Dolly's furniture polish and pine disinfectant. It had taken them a week to get home from Ireland. Both Beth and Mark were admitted to hospital and the police required Sheesha to work her way through a mountain of photos looking for the face of the man she had seen in the fire light.

'Perhaps you missed it,' said the sergeant hopefully when they came to the bottom of the pile.

'I'll never forget that face as long as I live,' replied Sheesha vehemently and she was quite pleased with the result of the photofit picture they made up.

All the tests showed that Beth's baby was completely unharmed, and Sheesha was forced to admit it certainly had a tenacious hold on life.

Mark's bang on the head did not seem to affect him half as much as the blow to his pride. He declared he would almost rather have died a hero's death than to have been rescued by a teenage girl, and dragged senseless from the scene by a pregnant woman and an elderly uncle! And the fact that God seemed to be getting all the credit did nothing for his self esteem. He was greatly comforted, however, by the ministrations of a blonde nurse with whom he was soon passionately in love.

'I know where I am with a girl like that,' he told Sheesha

when he came to see them off at the docks in Belfast. 'Boadiceas like you confuse me. Women should be women in my book.'

'It's time your book was burnt,' Sheesha had told him coldly, and turned her back on him and his simpering new girl friend.

'He's insufferable!' she thought as she slid off her bed and looked at herself in her bedroom mirror. 'I'll never let any man control me!' There, lying in a china dish on her dressing-table was the cross that her father had given her. She put out her hand to touch it, but then drew it hastily back. 'I don't want God to control me either,' she thought. 'I know He gave us power to get out of that Irish mess, but I'd still rather be my own boss – just for a little while longer. I want to become a great doctor just by my own efforts. My cottage is going to have to stay empty for a while longer.'

The exam results had been waiting for her when they arrived back. Dolly had refused to post them on, saying, 'I never bother the Doctor with anything when he's on holiday.' And when Sheesha opened the brown envelope she had been too pleased to be cross.

Sheesha had ten grade A's and could not help feeling if there had been a higher grade she would have got ten of those instead.

'I don't need God, or a man!' she thought smugly, but underneath she knew she needed love. 'Dad and Beth'll be proud of me now,' she thought as she gloated over her results, but Beth was absorbed in her baby and Michael was grieving over his cottage. Sheesha seemed happy enough to them, living in the little world of her bedroom, and they were frightened of making her swollen headed if they gave her too much encouragement so, because she made no demands on them they left her to live her own life.

There was a large 'For Sale' notice up outside Carolyn's house, and her mother said she was not coming back from Scotland until term began in two weeks' time. So Sheesha devoured books and sweets in large quantities and felt more lonely than ever before.

'Phone,' yelled Beth's voice one morning at the beginning of September.

'For me?' asked Sheesha in surprise, as she racked her brains to think of one single person in all the world who might bother to ring her.

'Hi!' said a cheery voice when she uncertainly lifted the receiver.

'Manda!' she squealed in utter delight. 'Where are you?'

'I'm home, got back yesterday. Why not come round now, Mum's working this morning.'

As she ran across the common she felt as if the sun had suddenly come out and was shining on her life. Everything would be alright now. 'I could help her with her physio and take her out in the wheelchair,' she thought happily. 'I'll give my whole life over to helping her, I'll prove how grateful I am.'

So many memories poured into Sheesha's mind as she walked into her old foster home. It was just the same. How could Manda's Mum and Beth possibly be sisters? They were so different. Not one detail was out of place in this house.

She had walked in through the back door, just as she always had in the old days, but as she stood in the middle of the gleaming kitchen, shyness suddenly engulfed her. Manda in a wheelchair – it didn't seem right somehow.

'Shut your eyes!' ordered Manda's voice from the sitting room, 'I'm going to give you a surprise.'

The surprise was so huge it nearly flattened her as the door opened and Manda *walked* into the kitchen! Well, walked was hardly the correct description of Manda's progress between two sticks. 'But anything's better than a wheelchair,' she beamed proudly. 'I'm going back to Gravely next week and I couldn't have faced it in one of those "degraders". Do you know,' she continued as they sipped their coffee, 'people never talk to you if you are in a wheelchair, they talk to the person who's pushing you. I cried out to God, and He really gave me the power to walk. The doctors never thought I would you know.'

'But if God could do that,' said Sheesha slowly, 'why didn't He have enough power to stop this happening to you in the first place?'

'I don't know,' grinned Manda. 'I've been asking that for months now. Mr Martin, he's the minister of your Dad's church, he came to see me in hopital and he said it's best not to ask *why* bad things happen to us, but *how* – how is God's power going to get me through this.'

'You've changed so much,' said Sheesha softly, 'you've grown up somehow,' and under her breath she added, 'if I stay around this girl I'm going to catch God like the measles, but I'm so happy I don't care.'

At that very minute a key was heard turning in the front door.

'I'm home early, love,' called Mrs Williams, 'I just couldn't leave you on your own . . . oh!' She stopped, frozen with horror in the doorway, as elegant and immaculate as ever. The mother Sheesha had so desperately wanted, the mother who had turned her out.

'*You*!' she gasped. '*How dare* you come here after all the trouble you caused our Manda. *Look*! Look at what you've done to her!'

'But I didn't do it to her deliberately,' cried Sheesha desperately.

'You made it happen with your witchcraft!' shouted Mrs Williams, 'just like you nearly broke up my marriage and got Manda arrested, let alone ruining her schoolwork and her swimming. You get out of this house now, before I ring the police!'

'Mum, don't,' protested Manda.

'You've got to rebuild your life from scratch, you can't do it with this thing hanging on you like a leech.' She flung open the front door and glared at Manda. 'Don't ever come back in here again, and Manda, you're not to go near your Auntie Beth's either. At least you'll both be in different schools. I won't have you two associating with each other in any way!'

The walk home across the common was a very different affair from the journey out and it finished inevitably in the sweet shop.

'Bang goes another friend!' thought Sheesha as she stuffed her mouth full of chocolate. 'Down the drain with Pippa and the Sherbet Lemons. Why does it always happen to me?'

A strange and very unusual thing happened to Sheesha on the morning of September 15th – she felt happy! The emotion was so alien to her that she was quite uneasy as she walked in through the wrought iron gates of the Sacred Heart. Before her the mellow old building rose graciously from its well-kept garden and Sheesha had the oddest feeling that she was coming home.

'Ah, there you are dear,' said Sister Gertrude as they met in the marble entrance hall, 'I really must congratulate you on your excellent exam results.' She was actually smiling and Sheesha had to drop her eyes and mumble something demure in order to stop an attack of the giggles.

'You'll be doing physics, chemistry, biology and maths in the sixth form, is that right?' continued the woman who had once called her a delinquent. 'I am sure that you will cope very well with the work load and do yourself justice in the exams.'

'And you and your school will take the credit,' thought Sheesha as she murmured, 'Thank you, Sister Gertrude.' Silently she added, 'I'll do so brilliantly I'll rock this old place to its foundations', as she made her way to the sixth form 'sitting room'.

It was a huge sunny room with low windows overlooking the gardens but no one came over to Sheesha and said 'Hello' when she jerked her way in through the door. 'I don't need this lot,' she thought, 'it's work that counts, not people. Let them rabbit on about their boyfriends and exotic holidays.' All the same her eyes wandered over the chattering crowd looking rather wistfully for Carolyn.

'Oh my dear,' said a loud and patronising voice, 'you *have* put on weight!' It was, naturally, Amy who had spoken and the crowd who surrounded her paused in their conversation to titter.

'If I were in a boys' school I'd knock you down,' thought Sheesha, but instead she said, 'And your acne's worse than ever', and felt she had scored an even more painful hit and she walked over to the window feeling considerably better.

'Hi,' said a voice from a great way below her.

'Carolyn!' she exclaimed as she looked down at her diminutive friend in horror. 'What have you done to yourself?'

Gone was the neat little china ornament, and in its place stood the kind of object never before seen in the Sacred Heart. 'I know we're allowed to wear our own gear in the Sixth, but isn't this going a bit far?'

The black baggy and ragged clothes looked as if she had filched them from the dustbin, her hair which was dyed black looked matted and unkempt and her eye makeup had to be seen to be believed.

'It's my new image,' giggled Carolyn. 'Sister Gertrude said I'll have to change it before tomorrow or leave – but it was worth it just to see her face.'

'You said you'd freak out,' gasped Sheesha, 'but I never thought you'd go this far.'

'Well I haven't quite decided what direction to freak into yet,' admitted Carolyn, 'but the new me has certainly riled up Mum and Sister Gertrude.'

'Your house is for sale,' said Sheesha in her usual direct way, 'you're not going to leave Fleetbridge like Pippa, are you?'

Carolyn flopped down onto the arm of a chair and lowering her voice to a tragic whisper she said, 'Mum and I have got to leave the house, and we're moving into a ghastly little Victorian terrace on the other side of town. Don't for goodness sake tell anyone here, they'd fall over their feet looking down their noses at me. I hate it all so much I nearly didn't come back to school this term. I thought I'd go up to London and try and get into modelling, but then I thought, why shouldn't Daddy pay the school fees, serves him right. But I won't do a stroke of work, that'll make them sorry.'

'Look what the cat brought in!' exclaimed Amy so loudly that all conversation died in the room. 'We've just bought your house, Caro, and I hear you're moving into the slums – but by the look of you,' she added scornfully, 'you live there already!'

Far away the bell began to ring, but as everyone surged towards the door Carolyn remained sitting like a granite statue.

'That is just too much!' she muttered. 'It was bad enough knowing we had to leave our lovely house, but to discover that Amy is going to be living in it – that's more than human sanity can stand. She'll probably have my bedroom, lie in my mauve bath, and swim in the pool

Daddy put in especially for me! It's too much. You wait till you see the rabbit hutch we'll be stuck in! It's no good, I'm just going to flip – I'm fed up! You escape into your work, don't you? That's not my scene. What do you suggest for me? The disco set, boys with a capital B?'

Sheesha looked down at her helplessly. 'Come on,' she said, 'Sister Gertrude'll have kittens if we're late for Assembly.'

'Those "gels" who are beginning today in the Sixth Form . . .'

The Headmistress launched herself into her annual pep talk not realising that the school knew it off by heart and were all reciting it with her *sotto voce* as they sat in their formal rows in the great school hall.

'. . . must realise that hard work and application now will affect the rest of their lives. It is our school tradition to send a high proportion of our pupils off to universities but during this year we shall be selecting our Oxbridge candidates. A small group of the most able of our "gels" will be specially prepared for the entrance examinations of Oxford and Cambridge. It is my ambition to have at least fifteen in the group this year . . .' Her voice faded away as Sheesha's mind became busy with her own thoughts. 'That's my freak out,' she thought, 'however vile life is, I've always got Oxford and medicine to look forward to. I'll work so hard, nothing else in life will matter.'

Chapter Eight

'I've discovered it!' Carolyn exploded into the library one Monday morning about a month into the term, her eyes positively glowing with excitement.

Sheesha put down her books and gazed at her in amazement. Poor Carolyn had been looking like a cat trapped in a washing machine for weeks. The move had been a terrible trauma to her, but Amy's occupation of her house and nasty comments had hurt far more, and Sheesha secretly thought her one and only friend was rapidly reaching breaking point. Was this the first sign? Was she high 'in a hypermanic euphoria'? Carolyn had certainly never looked as happy as this before.

'Discovered what?' whispered Sheesha, determined to humour the patient.

'Discovered my freak out. It's God – He's a lot less hassle than drugs and boys.'

'Religious mania,' thought Sheesha sadly. 'I must get Dad round to see her tonight.'

It was almost as if Carolyn had read her mind, when she continued, 'A couple of weeks ago I went round to your Dad's surgery, I felt so bad I thought I'd ask for some tranquillisers. Well, he said "before I give you pills, why not try church. There's one just over the road from your new house – it's where I go, you might love it." Well, that Sunday I tried it, and I met this friend of yours, Manda, the one who saved your life. She introduced me to masses of other people, and took me along to a sort of "do" at the Manse after the service. All people of our age, but they are so different! They really love God and they're all such fun. I've been to lots of things there during the past fortnight and last night in church I decided to freak out on God in a big way. I'm so happy I could zip open!'

'Well don't do it in the library,' said Sheesha crossly. 'Some of us want to work.'

'I thought you'd be pleased,' said Carolyn deflated. 'I can't think why you don't come along with your Dad. I just wish I'd discovered about all this years ago. Mum's livid with me, thinks I've gone nutty!'

'She's probably right,' growled Sheesha and turned back to her books. 'It won't last,' she thought. 'She'll get over it soon.'

But Sheesha was wrong. Over the next few weeks she witnessed an astounding change in Carolyn.

She had always secretly put her down as an empty-headed little bore, but suddenly she seemed to have a fascinating depth to her character and she was so happy it was like living next to a warm fire. It was really good fun to hang around school together, but Sheesha resolutely refused to go near her church or any of her odd set of friends.

It was a foggy November morning just a week before the General Election, and Sister Gertrude was making such a long speech in assembly that anyone would think she was standing for Parliament herself. 'As you know, "gels",' she boomed, 'today is a great day for Fleetbridge. We shall be honoured with a visit to the Town Hall by the Secretary of State for Northern Ireland. He will be making a major speech and I would have liked to have been able to encourage you all to go along and hear him. But there have been so many bomb scares and nasty threats that I must warn you to be careful, and I think as a school we should now rise and pray for his safety while he is in our town.'

'I'm going to hear Stanley Harcourt this evening,' said Carolyn as they filed out of the hall. 'I thought for one awful minute "Gerty" was going to put the Town Hall out of bounds.'

'You, going to a political meeting?' said Sheesha incredulously. 'I thought you and your lot were above that kind of thing.'

'We're not into prayer meetings and Bible study all the time,' grinned Carolyn, 'we thought we'd go along tonight just for a laugh.'

'You won't laugh very loudly if they plant a bomb under the platform,' commented Sheesha. 'Actually I was thinking of going myself,' she added, 'I've got quite interested in the Irish issue since last summer.'

'Come along with us,' suggested Carolyn. 'There's about ten of us going. Come to tea first. Would they mind at home?'

'Would they mind at home? Not much,' thought Sheesha bitterly. It would be a blessed relief just to be out of the house for an evening. Beth was feeling so much better she was unleashing all her Ward Sister energy on organising her new daughter. She labelled her efforts with all kinds of cliches such as 'bridging the gap', 'bonding', 'building meaningful relationships' and 'sharing'. All Sheesha wanted was peace to work and she heartily wished Beth could go back to being sick all day.

'I'll give them a ring at lunchtime,' she said. It would be fun to go out to a civilised tea with Carolyn's mother. Muffins by the fire and dainty fairy cakes, not greasy chips eaten off the kitchen table. But it was not to the Victorian rabbit hutch that Carolyn dragged her after school, but right into the lion's den. 'Mum's gone back to hairdressing in London,' explained Carolyn, 'So I have tea most days at the Manse,' and she opened the door of the rambling old house without so much as ringing the bell.

To Sheesha, Manses or Vicarages should be places of quiet prayer and contemplations, not a home for a menagerie of monkeys. As they entered the kitchen it seemed to Sheesha to contain a vast swirling crowd of people all talking at the tops of their voices. 'This is the nearest thing to hell that I've ever got into!' she told herself, and she was just edging her way backwards out of the door again when an ecstatic avalanche of love descended on her, and there was Manda hugging her and positively squealing with excitement.

'Whatever are you doing here?' enquired Sheesha feeling completely dazed.

'I've lived here since yesterday,' smiled Manda. 'Dad got a wonderful new job in Manchester, but I didn't want to move schools before the exams, so the Martins are letting me stay here until summer. That means we can see as much as we like of each other, without Mum breathing down our necks.'

The next hour was so full of new faces, names and noisy laughter that Sheesha only ever had a hazy confused memory of it later. Just two things stood in her memory, one was the happiness that seemed to bubble in all directions and the other was Mr Martin, the Minister. He was a quiet little man, who sat at the top of a huge table listening to what people said to him as if he was really interested.

'It is very special for us to have you here,' he said to Sheesha at the end of the meal as everyone darted about the room, helping with the washing up. 'We are deeply fond of your father and Beth, but we long to know you as well.'

'He means that,' thought Sheesha, who was never

deceived by a mask of politeness. 'This man reminds me strongly of Sherbet Lemons.'

'How will you get to the Town Hall, Manda?' asked the Minister's wife, 'It's too far for you to walk.'

'We'll push her in the wheelchair,' said a boy who seemed to have permanent hiccups, and a girl who never stopped giggling. Manda protested loudly, but had to give in when they threatened to leave her behind.

It was an extraordinary sensation for Sheesha to go out with a whole group of people. It was something she had never ever done before. Even on school outings she had always walked by herself. 'They are a strange lot,' she thought, as she found herself watching them curiously. Could they really be this happy without drugs or alcohol? And why were they so nice to her? After all she was an outsider, yet she felt they genuinely wanted her to be there, and Sheesha was not accustomed to feeling wanted.

It was really Manda who fascinated her the most, however. She was in her element, obviously the centre of the group, with everyone wanting to talk to her and walk along beside the wheelchair. 'How she's changed!' thought Sheesha. 'She'll never be the little dog I can kick about any more – she's a superstar round here.' The thought began to irritate her more and more as they walked towards the centre of the town. Even Carolyn was a different person with these people. She seemed to sparkle with life and fun. 'There are two more people who seem to have got their power to cope with their lives from God,' she thought, 'but they're not going to suck me into all this. I've got something better to do with my life.'

'Why does that boy keep hiccupping?' she demanded as the constant burps began to irritate her.

'He's an ex-junkie,' explained Carolyn, 'but the heroin damaged his stomach. He's living at the Manse while he gets himself organised.'

It seemed that the police were taking the bomb threats as seriously as Sister Gertrude and as they neared the Town Hall every second person seemed to be wearing a helmet.

'We'll never get the wheelchair up all those steps,' announced Manda when they reached the imposing but inconvenient municipal facade.

'You can go in the back entrance,' said a helpful policeman. 'You reach it by going down the alleyway at the side of the building. We have cordoned off the whole area for security reasons, but we've been told to allow disabled people and their attendants to use that entrance.'

'No IRA men'll be able to get past this lost,' giggled Carolyn when they reached the well guarded barrier at the entrance to the narrow street. 'How many of us will they count as attendants?'

The sergeant who was on duty treated them all like royalty. 'He's one of the church deacons,' explained Carolyn. 'He looks funny in his uniform.'

'I can personally vouch for all these young people,' beamed the Sergeant. 'You go on in and enjoy yourselves,' he added, patting Manda on the shoulder and removing the barrier as he waved them past into the dark little street.

'We'll be late,' hiccupped John, rocketing the wheelchair off into the shadows. It was then that Sheesha felt the stone in her shoe. 'If I don't get it out, I'll ruin another pair of tights,' she thought, and stopped to deal with it. The gap widened between her and the group who were soon out of sight round a bend in the alley. It was eerie here alone with the fog smothering the only street light. A solitary car was parked under the muffled amber light with its engine ticking over gently. An orange disabled badge was stuck in the back window making the powerful man at the wheel look strangely out of place. Sheesha always noticed the tiny details that most other people missed.

'These orange badges are a racket,' she thought as she looked down suspiciously into the man's face. Suddenly she stopped, jarred by surprise. The face that looked at her was only too familiar, and her stomach lurched with panic. What was this Irishman doing in Fleetbridge on the very day the Secretary of State for Northern Ireland was making his big speech? This must be a getaway car, the disabled badge a perfect cover. Had the sinister occupant of some other wheelchair already gone into the Town Hall? Ahead Manda and Carolyn would be entering the building, she must warn them. But it was too late, the man had remembered her face too, and he had seen her startled look of recognition. The door of the car burst open, knocking her backwards against the wall of the public library. Suddenly she was looking down the barrel of his gun for the second time in her life. Wildly she looked up the alley, but the others had disappeared and she could no longer hear their cheerful voices. The police barrier and the friendly Sergeant were also out of sight.

'If you scream, I'll shoot yer!' hissed the man as if he could read her mind.

'I can't use God's power this time,' she thought wildly, 'not when I've deliberately decided to live my own life. I'll have to rely on myself this time.' She brought her knee up sharply aiming for the man's groin, but he was expecting her attack and dodged it on lightening quick boxer's feet. Suddenly Sheesha was reeling from the shock of a heavy blow to the mouth. For a moment she thought her neck must be broken, and the salty taste of blood filled her mouth. Before she could gasp for breath she was bundled into the back of the car just like a helpless, useless woman on a crummy TV drama. Was this man who had destroyed her father's cottage also going to destroy the only friends she had?

But help was on its way from two directions at once. High on the roof of the public library two policemen had seen the whole incident through their binoculars and instantly they were descending the marble stairs two at a time. At just the same moment an unwieldy army lead by a general in a wheelchair began to charge down the alley. They had rounded the corner in search of Sheesha just in time to see her being flung into the back of the car.

'Leave her alone,' shouted Manda just as two of the policemen hurtled out of the side door of the library. Both rescue parties collided with terrible force and were soon tangled together in a hopeless mass of arms, legs and spinning wheels. Sheesha and the Irishman both seized their chance to escape, and as he dived into the front seat of the car, she sprang out onto the pavement. The police Sergeant was soon using some very undeacon-like language as he watched a car zoom through his carefully constructed barrier and escape off into the fog.

'Let him go,' shouted Sheesha, as the two constables from the roof picked themselves up and began running after the red tail lights. 'That was only the getaway car, Stanley Harcourt is in terrible danger, you must evacuate the building.'

Soon the whole side street was swarming with police talking into their radios. The car containing the Secretary of State was only one block away when it swerved suddenly and turned in the opposite direction, much to the astonishment of its important occupant. The Town Hall was cleared in minutes while a team of policemen and dogs began their search. No one noticed a little old lady pushing a little old man in a wheelchair. They had been standing with the large crowd at the bottom of the Town Hall steps, waiting to wave as the great man got out of his car. When the Police began to clear the spectators they hurried away with everyone else, leaving the remains of their little picnic wrapped in a Tesco bag in a litter bin nearby. It was not until all the fuss had died down and the police had given up their fruitless search for a bomb that a hungry tramp, scavenging for his supper in the litter bin, discovered a gun with a silencer under the egg sandwiches. But long before he had taken his discovery to the police station the frail little couple were safely on the London bound train, talking loudly about the visit they were making to their married daughter in Islington.

The evening had turned out to be one of the nicest of Sheesha's life, as she, and the ten members of the church youth group sat in the police station waiting room. They were treated like VIPs by all the top ranking officers of the local force, and, as Sheesha told the story of her previous encounter with the terrorist, their deferential manner caused enormous amusement among the group. 'You wait,' laughed Carolyn, 'they'll get the Mayor himself in here soon to lick your boots, and the Prime Minister will follow!' They whiled away the evening answering questions, drinking free coke and laughing hysterically at jokes that weren't even funny. It felt wonderful having everyone liking her, and tomorrow when the story broke in the media she would be a national celebrity. But then the blow fell. The door of the waiting room opened and in walked the Chief Inspector and Michael, followed by a posse of plain clothes policemen.

'We want you to know,' said the Chief Inspector as he shook her hand violently, 'that your recognition of the man in the car quite obviously saved the life of Mr Harcourt. We are deeply grateful to you, but we also feel that your life could now be in great danger.' A cold feeling of dread began to creep into Sheesha, freezing the warm frothy happiness that had been there before. 'This Irishman has no police record as yet, and he knows that you, and you alone could identify him. Therefore I feel that it is vital that you do not talk to the media, or give them your name and address or allow yourself to be photographed. We *must* keep your part in tonight's affair completely secret for your own protection. Do you *all* understand me?' he inquired, glaring at the youth group. 'If you talk about what really happened tonight, your friend may lose her life. I am very much afraid she will be in grave danger until this man is safely in custody.'

It would have been nice, thought Sheesha, as she drifted off to sleep that night, to have had her face on every TV screen in the land, and her name in every paper. It would have been lovely to have Sister Gertrude making a speech about her from the platform in Assembly, and it would have been fun to walk down the street and know that heads were turning and fingers pointing. To be famous for doing something helpful would have made a pleasant change, but as the memory of the rugged face of the man she had twice foiled floated into her mind, she shivered. Her lips were sore and her teeth hurt badly, and she was afraid of physical pain. 'I know in my bones I'll see him again,' she thought. 'I wasn't very much good on my own without God's power tonight. Where would I have been now if Manda and the policemen hadn't come? I think perhaps it would be fun to be with that gang again.'

Chapter Nine

'You are invited as guest of honour to a secret celebration
in the Manse at 4 pm on Sunday. The Official Secrets Act
will be upheld at all times.'

Sheesha recognised Manda's handwriting on the card
that Carolyn passed to her as she entered the Sacred Heart
on Friday morning.

'You must come, you're the hero of the hour!' she
laughed. 'Everyone who was with us at the Town Hall has
clubbed together to make you a presentation. They all think
you're wonderful. Your Dad and Beth are invited too.'

It was a strange experience for Sheesha to be the centre
of attention, and as they sat round the huge table gloating
over their adventure and eating slices of the massive cake
Mrs Martin had baked especially, she suddenly felt
accepted. Mr Martin made a speech at the end and
presented Sheesha with a Bible. All their signatures were
on the flyleaf—'To our Hush Hush Heroine' it said, and
she felt strangely pleased with it. 'These people really do
seem to like me,' she thought, and when someone
suggested she went to church that evening it seemed the
most natural thing in the world just to say yes. Had she
known what was going to happen that night she would
have gone straight home to bed.

As they walked out of the Manse it seemed as if the
whole of Fleetbridge was converging on the church.
People were flocking from all directions.

114

'Is something special happening?' she asked Carolyn.

'Oh no, it's always like this on Sunday evenings, if you don't get here twenty minutes early you don't get a seat!'

The back of the church seemed to be reserved for young people and Sheesha felt her shyness slip away as she found herself waving and smiling at many old 'Gravely' faces. People thought nothing of reaching over two pews just to bang her on the shoulder and tell her she was welcome.

'Why did I get so steamed up the first time I came here?' she thought, 'but perhaps it's having Carolyn and Manda on either side of me.' The unfriendly world of Amy and the Sixth form seemed suddenly very unreal.

'I could belong here,' she thought as everyone around her began to sing. Suddenly she 'saw' in her mind the little cottage by the two rivers in Ireland. Empty, clean and furnished. But hiding behind the beech trees and boulders she could see the sinister masters she had once served so effectively. 'People who leave their cottages empty are asking for trouble,' echoed Mark's voice. Would hate, bitterness and anger invade her again one day unless she was filled up with God? And could she really manage her own life without His power? 'I could give myself over to God right here and now,' she thought. 'He might even hlep me to love Beth and her baby.'

But Sheesha was forgetting she had once been a witch, and Satan, her old master did not want to lose her forever.

'Let us pray,' said Mr Martin from the front of the crowded church.

'Here goes then,' thought Sheesha as she bowed her head with everyone else, but it was at that very moment that things began to go wrong. A frightful feeling of panic hit her with the same cruel force as the fist of the Irishman.

'You're mine!' screamed a voice in her head. 'I won't let you go!' Manda and Carolyn looked at her in horror as she

115

gasped for breath – ice cold hands seemed to be round her neck – and she began to struggle frantically.

'I'm not yours!' she shouted. Every head in the church turned in amazement and Mr Martin's voice stopped abruptly. The same feeling of suffocation that she had felt the first time she had come to this church was closing in on her, and she struggled to her feet. 'Get out of here,' ordered the inner voice. 'These people are dangerous.' In her terror she screamed once and then again, while the congregation gazed at her in paralysed horror. Even through her panic she felt the shame and embarrassment of being a public spectacle and her father's expression of twisted concern as he jumped up from his place. Out of the pew she stumbled totally disregarding the feet she trampled on in her panic. Sobbing with fright she ran up the aisle pushing roughly past the people who stood up to help her, and hurling herself through the swing doors she plunged down the steps to freedom. History seemed to be repeating itself.

She did not care where she ran, she was still too frightened to think, and the memory of those cold hands on her throat made her shudder. People were running after her calling her name, they were gaining on her, she must get away. The busy main road was in front of her with its reassuring street lights and bustling traffic. She ran into the road without looking. Someone behind her screamed, headlights dazzled her eyes and the squeal of brakes and protesting tyres deafened her ears. Something hit her hard on the shoulder and this time there was no one to push her out of the way.

It suited her sense of drama nicely to wake up in hospital. But it was a slight anti-climax to discover that she was not dead.

'Just a bit of concussion and a lot of bruises,' said her

father who was sitting next to her in the casualty department. 'They'll keep you in overnight, but you'll be fine in the morning. The bumper of a lorry just clipped you.'

'That's the very last time I ever go to that church,' muttered Sheesha. 'I made a fool of myself completely.'

'What happened to you in church was quite normal,' smiled her father. 'When someone has been as useful to Satan as you were, he naturally puts up a massive fight to keep them. You mustn't listen to his lies, you don't belong to him any more. We could pray right now, and release you forever from his power.'

'I'm sick of being torn in half by all this hassle,' quavered Sheesha. 'I just want to forget everything and everyone, and get on with my work in peace.' And closing her eyes, she shut her father's sad face out of her mind.

A whole month had passed since that fateful visit to church. It had been a very strange month, she thought as she lay in the bath at ten o'clock on the morning of Christmas Eve. Not a month she would like to live through again.

The X-rays and tests showed clearly that there was very little physical damage done by her argument with the lorry, but she came out of hospital feeling ghastly.

'Delayed shock,' said Beth, but Sheesha knew it was fear. Fear of the Irishman – but also of the deadly crushing power of Satan. So she shut her bedroom door firmly on the world and buried her fear under a mountain of books. Manda rang frequently at first. And deep inside, Sheesha longed to respond to the friendliness in her voice, but she dared not. Finally, even Manda got the message that she really did want to be left alone.

Mr Martin came round to see her one evening, but she told Beth she had a headache and couldn't come downstairs. 'I just don't get you,' complained Carolyn one day at school when Sheesha had refused yet again to go with her to church.

'Why don't you all just leave me to get on with my own life,' Sheesha snapped and she even felt pleased when they broke up for the holidays. The only good thing about fear, she thought, as she lay in the warm bath was that it completely prevented her from eating, and she had lost a stone and a half. Her anorexia had returned.

She poured in some more hot water and luxuriated in the unusual silence of the house. Beth had gone up to the hospital for an ante-natal check up, her father would be rocketting round Fleetbridge, trying to persuade his patients they were going to be miraculously healthy over the holiday, and Dolly was lying in her sister's house with her broken ankle encased in a plaster cast of gigantic proportions. It had all happened yesterday, and Sheesha smiled as she remembered the delicious drama. Beth had left her slippers on the stairs, and Dolly who was unable to see her feet past the vast expanse of her stomach had slipped on them and crashed from the top to the bottom of the elegant staircase, swearing dreadfully all the way down.

'If you weren't so * * * * untidy, Mrs Davidson,' she had roared as the two sweating ambulancemen hauled her onto a stretcher, 'this would never have happened.'

'Of course it wasn't funny really,' thought Sheesha as she turned off the hot tap with her feet. Without Dolly's daily visits she would have to do far more to help during the holidays. Beth was being quite impossible over her preparations for Christmas. She had been whirling round like a spinning top for days, shopping, wrapping parcels, and cooking goodies that Sheesha was terrified she'd have to eat, and then last night to cap it all, she had 'decorated'. To Beth that meant covering the already cluttered house with tatty sprigs of holly, plastic Father Christmasses and lurid coloured paper chains.

'Darling, you're doing far too much!' complained Michael when he had come in from evening surgery and found Beth up a step ladder. At that moment the paper-chain she was trying to hang disintegrated and sailed dismally to the floor. Beth was tired and strained after the traumas of the day and her sense of humour had been completely lost under the mountain of her activity.

'How can I help doing too much if your daughter won't do anything but sit reading all day!' she shouted. 'Why don't you tell her to give me a hand,' she added, and burst into tears.

Sheesha lay in the bath, remembering how she stood in the doorway, silently challenging her father to a dual. He merely looked uncomfortable and she had sensed he hated the decorations as much as she did.

'If she wants to make this place look like a cheap, run-down pub, why should I help her. I hate Christmas anyway,' she had said, opening the attack.

'I think it all looks very nice,' lied her father, helping Beth down the ladder. 'But I'm sure we don't need any more,' he added hastily.

'But I've still got all the mince pies to make this evening,' sniffed Beth.

'Well, why not give Sheesha a cookery lesson. You could both do them together.'

'Why make any of the beastly things at all,' Sheesha had added coldly. 'I won't eat them, Beth shouldn't eat them, and if you must have some, we'll buy a box of them at the shop.'

'All my life I've dreamed of having a home of my own at Christmas,' sobbed Beth pathetically. 'I wanted to do all the proper housewifely things, and I haven't even started to get supper.'

'Come on then,' smiled Michael. 'We'll go and get a snack at MacDonalds and then have an early night. Next

Christmas the baby will be old enough to enjoy all the decorations. We can go to town on them then.' Sheesha had refused to go out with them, and then had been hurt by the look of relief she thought she detected on both of their faces.

The thought that Beth and her father did not really want her made her feel sick, and the idea of the baby enjoying the Christmas tree lights accentuated her loneliness.

Somewhere in the house the phone was ringing. 'Let it ring,' thought Sheesha, it wouldn't be for her. After that ghastly fiasco in church a month ago, she had been branded a witch and disgraced herself in front of a whole church full of people. 'I wish I'd never gone to that Manse,' she thought miserably. 'At least I was reasonably contented on my own before I saw how different life could be.'

The phone was still ringing. Obviously It was someone who knew she was in the house, and wasn't going to be ignored. With a sigh she rolled herself out of the bath and wrapped a towel round her dripping body.

'Hello!' she said when she reached the phone at the end of the trail of her own wet footprints.

'It's Beth,' said a voice that did not sound like Beth's at all. 'I can't reach your Dad, he's out on his calls. Something's gone wrong. I'm still at the hospital, they want to keep me in. My blood pressure has shot up, they say I've been overdoing things and they want me to rest completely.' Sheesha managed not to say 'I told you so', and Beth continued. 'Can you bring my stuff straight up here? I've made a list of what I need.'

That Christmas holiday was the happiest Sheesha had ever known. Apart from his visits to Beth, and his time in church, she had her father entirely to herself. They sat by the fire in the lounge, reading in companionable silence, while they listened to all their favourite music. He talked to her about medical things as if she was already a doctor and Sheesha realised how completely happy she could be if only Beth had never existed. The fear that had dominated her went into hibernation as the peaceful days grew into weeks, and when Michael said, 'I'm afraid they are going to keep her in until after the baby arrives', Sheesha had to bury her face in her books so he would not see her smile of delight. A niece of Dolly's came in every day to 'Do' for them, and without Beth to 'undo' all her efforts she soon had the house back to the elegant order of its pre-Beth days. Breakfasts were again set in the dining room, and the egg cups were polished until they gleamed. Sheesha looked up the sections on 'Toxaemia' of pregnancy in her father's medical books, and gloated over figures of mother and baby mortality. 'How wonderful life would be, if only . . .' But one day, with the sudden jarring shock of a violent thunderstorm in the middle of a lazy summer afternoon, Beth came home, and of course she did not come alone. In the carry cot came Edward and everyone said he was the image of his father. Sheesha wondered sourly how Michael could possibly look so inordinately pleased by being likened to a hairy beetroot, but she did not say so.

Their lives went to pieces within hours of Beth's return. She had a major row with Dolly's niece, who gave in her notice on the spot. 'Never mind,' said Beth, 'if you two both give a hand, we'll manage fine.'

'Of course we will,' smiled Michael fondly, while Sheesha ground her teeth.

The hope that the baby might not be intelligent was shattered very soon for Sheesha. Edward had an uncanny way of knowing exactly when it was time for a meal to be dished up, and he would wake instantly, and demand his feed. Saucepans boiled over and casseroles dried up in the oven while he took at least an hour to get through his bottle. The undivided attention of both his parents were required while he played around with the teat, and filled quantities of nappies whith unmentionable unpleasantness. When the bottle was finally empty, there was no gurgling in his cot for this monster. He stage-managed wind for at least a further hour, and bawled until the house shuddered, and both his parents dashed about trying every remedy their medical training had taught them. Nothing worked. 'He just likes the fuss,' thought Sheesha. Wherever she went in the house she fell over baby equipment, or pails of dirty nappies, while the sour smell of the last feed he had sicked up over the velvet sofa hung heavily in the air. If she played her music in her room, she was told it would wake him, but no one cared that she was kept awake most nights by his angry screams.

'Had your nose put out of joint,' said one of Beth's numerous cronies, 'that's why you're looking so sulky.'

'Step this way with the gold, frankincense and myrrh,' thought Sheesha as she saw from her bedroom window yet another little group of baby worshippers padding up the drive.

'Life is quite intolerable,' she sighed as she turned back to her biology essay, 'and it won't get better. Soon he'll be saying cute little things, following Dad round the garden at weekends, and he'll be so spoilt he'll be insufferable! "Men always want a son!" But I'll show them all that a woman can be the greatest doctor in the world.'

Chapter Ten

It was the Irishman who was creeping through the darkness towards her bed. His great icy hands were round her neck. She tried to scream but no sound would come. No, he wasn't the Irishman, he was Satan himself, pulling her back into His Kingdom of darkness. 'Today everything's going to end,' screamed a voice. . . and she woke up!

Had all that really only been another of her nightmares? 'Dreams really do come true sometimes,' she thought. As she slid out of bed she found her teeth were chattering. But it was not cold, the warm spring sunshine was streaming in through chinks in her curtains, yet the voice kept booming menacingly in her head. 'Today everything's going to end.' 'I felt a bit like this a year ago,' she thought when she realised it was April 26th. Could it really be a whole year since they were married? She had felt a premonition of disaster that day too, and how right she had been. She had lost Pippa and Sherbet Lemons, her father and the hope that Beth would be the mother she had always longed to have. 'Everything's going to end today!' She shivered violently as the events of the previous evening washed back into her mind. Would they come and put her in a mental hospital? She and Beth had had a terrible row but this one had not ended in a cut head and laughter.

Beth had changed radically since Edward's birth three

months before. Life with a real baby was not quite like her daydreams had depicted. Edward's constant, round-the-clock screams had worn her out and crumbled her professional efficiency. She felt depressed, bewildered and completely humiliated by Sheesha's refusal of all her overtures of friendship. Outgoing extroverts seldom understand the need for solitude, so she put Sheesha's withdrawal into her private world down to a fit of sulks. Once she would have laughed off her daughter's moods, but somehow her sense of humour had been mislaid beneath a pile of dirty nappies.

'How can I possibly do my physics with that baby bawling continuously?' demanded Sheesha, when she burst into the kitchen the evening before. It had been the end of the road for Beth's patience.

'What do you suppose it's like for me, having to listen to him all day long?' she shouted as she burst into tears. 'Your father will be in from surgery any minute, and if I go and pacify Edward the meal will never be cooked. Couldn't you be helpful for once and grill these sausages?' It was the 'for once' and the lack of a 'please' that caused Sheesha to refuse, but she actually sounded ruder than she really meant to be.

'I don't like eating myself, so why should I cook your food?' she finished.

'You're right,' shouted Beth. 'You don't like eating, look at you.' And she pulled at the baggy sweater that Sheesha wore to conceal her emaciated body. 'You're an advanced Anorexic! I've been so absorbed in Edward that I haven't been paying enough attention to what you eat. Just how little do you weigh now? You ought to be in hospital.'

'Keep your interfering nose out of my life,' snarled Sheesha dangerously. Suddenly Beth wasn't angry any more as concern sprang into her eyes. 'I've been so depressed, I haven't realized, but you're ill, you need the discipline of a psychiatric ward. I know, I've nursed hundreds of anorexics.'

Her concern was professional and it was also very real, but to Sheesha she simply sounded mean and cruel as she continued, 'We used to take everything off our patients, all their own clothes, books, radios, the lot, and then we'd keep them on total bed rest. Poor kids, they were bored out of their minds. When they had gained a few pounds they were allowed to get up and go to the loo, a few more pounds and they had their own clothes back, then their other possessions one by one as they gained weight.'

'It sounds barbarous,' exlaimed Sheesha.

'We had to be,' said Beth. 'Anorexics are up to every deceitful trick you can imagine to avoid eating their food or vomiting it all up after a meal. We even had to feed them by force sometimes. I really think hospital is the only answer for you. I'll talk to your father tonight. It's the lack of food that's making you so awkward. You're starving yourself to a dangerous level.'

'You'd love to get rid of me, wouldn't you,' Sheesha had stormed, 'and spoil my chances of being a doctor. Getting me into mental hospital would solve both problems. Well, you won't take away my home, or Oxford and medicine. I'll spoil your fun right now!' And sitting down at the table she had stuffed herself with slices of bread and jam. Beth had picked Edward from his pram and walked out of the room with a look of smug triumph on her face.

'How I hate her!' growled Sheesha as she forced the memory of the past evening out of her mind. 'She'll feel she's won whether I eat or starve.' Hate! Once it had ruined her life, was it doing the same thing again? Had fear and hate climbed back into the empty cottage and repossessed it? She thrust the thought from her mind, and began to get herself dressed.

She did not want to eat any breakfast, the bread and jam still sitting heavily in her tummy. 'But I won't give them the chance to lock me away,' she thought as she rammed some bread into the ancient toaster.

Last night's supper things littered the table and the pans in the sink were covered in congealed grease. The sight was enough to kill the appetite of a heavyweight boxer, but she had fainted in the chemistry lab the day before, and she knew it had been due to lack of food.

It was while she was fiddling with the toaster that had decided to stick once again that Michael walked into the room. Yet another sleepless night with the baby had shredded his nerves to ribbons, and the chaos of the room affected him in exactly the same way as it had revolted his daughter. He had left a tearful Beth upstairs in bed, complaining about how awkward and unhelpful Sheesha was being, and suddenly it seemed to his tired mind that all the mess that surrounded him was Sheesha's fault.

'This house is a disgrace!' he barked.

'I agree with you,' said Sheesha as the toast leapt up and hit her in the eye.

'So why don't you do something about it, you lazy slut!' He had never shouted at her before, and he regretted the words the moment he heard himself speak them, but for Sheesha they were as painful and as unexpected as gunfire. She stood looking at him, stunned and humiliated as she tried to wipe the toast crumbs from her eye. And then the anger came, and all the hurt and resentment of the last three months erupted like a volcano.

'I'm not the lazy slut round here,' she screamed. 'She's upstairs and you were fool enough to marry her.'

When a gentle person loses their temper they usually lose it completely, simply because they have not had practice in keeping it, and Michael burst across the room and slapped Sheesha's cheek with a force that astonished him.

126

'Last year,' sobbed Sheesha, 'you couldn't do enough for me – your long-lost daughter. Now you expect me to do all the dirty work and when I refuse you knock me about and threaten to shove me in a mental hospital.' She saw her father wince, but before he could say anything she had slammed the front door behind her with a force that shook the house.

The only tiny chink in the cloud of misery that surrounded her was the thought that when she got to school Carolyn would be there. 'She'll know just how I feel,' she thought as she walked across the common. 'Her parents are ghastly too. She at least will understand.'

But Carolyn did not understand. 'I'm getting sick of you,' she said when Sheesha had finished growling her tale of woe in the Sixth form sitting room. 'If you had my parents for a few days you'd realise how lucky you are. I see lots of your Dad and Beth at church and they're lovely, but you're breaking them up by the way you act towards them.' Sheesha, completely robbed of speech, stood gaping at her one and only friend, but Carolyn had not finished. 'I don't know how much longer I can go on wasting my time knocking about with you when all you do is deliberately turn your back on God and everything that's nice in life. Manda's right, you only enjoy being unhappy.'

'So you and Manda discuss me, do you?' said Sheesha in a dangerously quiet way.

'Yes we do,' said Carolyn gently, 'and we also pray for you.'

'So you're sick of me, are you? Don't want to be my friend any more 'cos you and Manda have got each other now? Is that it?' Carolyn never had time to answer before Sheesha had launched herself across the room, like an angry tigress springing on her prey. Startled girls scattered in all directions, dropping books and overturning chairs in their flight, and what would have become of fragile little Carolyn if Sister Barbara had not been passing the door at just that moment, no one ever knew.

'Stop that at once you wretched "gel"!' she shrieked as her bony claw clutched at Sheesha's hair. 'You should never have been allowed to come to a nice school like this, you are a bad influence, you're rotten all through.'

'How dare you say that!' shouted Sheesha as she let Carolyn go and turned on an older enemy.

'I beg your pardon?' demanded the outraged nun.

'You heard,' growled Sheesha.

'I am pained to have to remind you that at a school like this we do not expect our "gels" to brawl or speak rudely to members of staff, but when one remembers that you came to us from Parkfield, one can hardly feel surprised.'

'Sometimes I wish I was still at Parkfield,' shouted Sheesha, 'at least there we didn't have to put up with ugly old hypocrites like you!'

Amid a gasp of horror, the scraggy nun swept out of the room to carry her triumphant spite to Sister Gertrude's office. She had long waited for this pleasureable moment.

'They'll suspend you for that,' said a pious girl who was always talking about her call to the convent life.

'I couldn't care less,' snorted Sheesha and added a word that the future nun had never heard before.

The summons to Sister Gertrude's room did not come until the middle of the afternoon, and the long wait seemed to Sheesha like calculated cruelty. Carolyn never looked in her direction once, and she realized just how bleak life was going to be without a single friend. What if they really did suspend her, that would spell the end of everything all right, just as the dream voice had predicted.

As she walked down the corridor in Sister Gertrude's direction she contorted her face into an expression of

128

penitence. Hate and anger would *not* keep ruining her life, she would eat humble pie even if it made her sick. But the contrite expression was wiped from her face when she saw Sister Barbara standing by her superior, her 'claws' folded smugly in front of her and a look of sheer malice on her shrunken face.

'I think you owe Sister Barbara an apology,' said the Headmistress coldly.

'I think she owes me one,' Sheesha found herself saying. In all the difficulties of her unhappy life she had always protected herself by anger, and the habit was a hard one to break.

'You will be suspended from school until you do apologise,' continued the icy voice.

'You can't do that!' stormed Sheesha. 'With the Oxbridge entrance exam in the autumn, I can't afford to miss any school.'

'I'm not sure we shall be putting you in the Oxbridge group after all,' said Sister Gertrude.

'But I'm going to my father's college in Oxford to read medicine,' said Sheesha uneasily.

'I doubt if any medical school will accept you,' said the Headmistress with finality.

'Why?' demanded Sheesha, 'I've been getting phenomenally high marks.'

'They will be looking for much more than academic excellence. They are looking for maturity, and you have hardly displayed that quality today.'

'But I'm not feeling well, I fainted yesterday. Surely anyone can have one bad day.'

'They will be looking for people with wide interests and the ability to get on well with other people. You don't do any kind of sport, you're not involved in dramatics or voluntary work, you're not even a Prefect. When we come to fill in the UCCA forms, what will we find to say about you?'

'But I don't have time for all those babyish things,' snapped Sheesha.

'I'm sorry, but unless you appear as a very caring, interested and involved kind of person, medicine will be out of the question. In fact with your antisocial outlook it will be hard to find any career for you whatsoever.'

Sheesha was not listening any more. The faces of the two nuns were swimming before her eyes. The one driving force of her life had been her certainty that she was on the road to medicine. Never in all her worst nightmares had she ever thought that her future was in any doubt. If she wasn't going to be a doctor then she did not want to live. Was she going to faint again? 'I'm not going to make a fool of myself in front of these two old crows,' she thought and fumbled her way to the door, looking like a dying man who has been shot several times in the heart.

'*Do not* come back until you are ready to apologise!' came Sister Barbara's shrill voice.

'There's no point in ever coming back now,' muttered Sheesha and tottered away down the corridor.

The common felt desolate as she picked her way blindly between the gorse bushes, not really caring where she went. There was no one in all the world to whom she could go now. She was utterly alone, and nothing but empty blackness lay ahead.

'You might as well be dead,' said the voice in her head, so distinctly that she found herself looking over her shoulder to see if someone had actually whispered it in her ear. 'Go and finish it all now, no one will care.'

'I know how I'll do it,' she thought, stopping still in the muddy path. The pot of sleeping pills were still in the cupboard in the second bathroom which she and Dolly shared. Dolly had left them behind when she left, and Sheesha had used the odd one or two when the baby had been extra noisy at night.

'I'll go back and do it now,' she thought, 'the sooner I'm out of this world the better.'

She opened the front door, bracing herself for the onslaught of screams or the tactless comments of visitors, but the house was as silent as the grave in which she hoped she would soon be lying.

If she had only known what her father and Beth were doing at that moment she might not have gone upstairs to the bathroom cupboard with quite the same tragic purpose.

Chapter Eleven

Beth had come downstairs that morning as soon as she heard the front door slam. Her husband was sitting at the cluttered kitchen table, his head in his hands, and his shoulders slumped in despair.

'I heard all that from upstairs,' she said, 'that girl certainly can take the giggles out of life.'

'Can't you understand how serious this is?' said Michael desperately. 'I never thought it would be so difficult to be a father.'

'Come on, cheer up, said Beth, putting on her bright and cheerful mask. 'It's our wedding anniversary, remember?' Michael covered his face again and remembered. But remembering hurt. What a nightmare of a year it had been. Whatever was he going to do?

'You're a wonderful father,' said Beth gently, laying her hand on his shoulder. 'It's me she's angry with. Whatever I do or say is wrong. I just can't handle this constant wall of hate, and I just don't know how much longer I can go on living with it.'

'I don't know how long any of us can go on with anything,' said Michael bleakly and rushed off to his surgery.

'Everything's going wrong!' muttered Beth when she was alone and the smile slipped from her face. The angry screams were beginning again in the nursery above, and wearily she pulled herself up the stairs. 'Life never does seem to turn out the way you expect.'

She was crying as she entered the nursery and at first she felt too tired to lift Edward out of his cot. She just stood looking down at his angry red face in a kind of stupor. Suddenly the noise subsided and looking up into his mother's face he smiled enormously. He had his father's smile and its effects were just the same.

'I love you,' whispered Beth as she lifted him into her arms, 'you drive me mad, but I love you.' On the way to the kitchen she passed the door of Sheesha's bedroom. The door stood open and she went quietly inside. 'That's the difference,' she thought. 'I love Edward however awful he is, but I don't love Sheesha.'

The thought nagged her all day like a toothache, and by the end of the afternoon she was so miserable she put Edward into his pram and pushed him over to the Manse.

'I need help,' she said when she was settled in Mr Martin's shabby study. 'I've always thought our daughter Meggan was such a huge problem, and if only she could change everything would be fine, but I discovered today it's really me who's got to change. Can we pray about it?'

Michael had sat at his desk feeling like a robot. Patient after patient sat down in the chair beside him, their lips moved, their heads wagged and he wrote them a prescription, but the office cleaner would have done a better job as a doctor that day.

'It's my teenage daughter, Doctor, she's impossible! But I know you'll be able to help me.' The words cut into Michael's brain like a surgeon's knife.

'I'm sorry,' he said smiling ruefully, 'you've come to the wrong man.'

'He's three months old Doctor, and he just won't stop crying, night or day.' The next patient had come in and was looking at him appealingly. 'Whatever can I do?'

'I could tell you a hundred things to do, but probably

none of them will work,' said Michael, 'all I can give you is my sympathy.'

'Doctor, I think my marriage is breaking up, what shall I do?'

This patient was too much for poor Michael, and he blew his nose loudly. 'You come to our church, don't you?' he replied. 'Why don't you pray about it?'

'Do you really think God could help?' asked the woman doubtfully.

'Yes,' replied Michael slowly, 'I really do.' He wrote her a prescription for tranquillizers and as she walked out of the room he found himself doodling the word 'hypocrite' on his notepad. 'Why don't I take my own advice?' he thought, as he slid into his car to start his home calls. 'Hypocrite, that's what I am.'

Mr Martin and Beth were both somewhat surprised to see Michael walk into the study. 'I just can't cope with the way I feel inside,' said Michael, flopping down on the old leather sofa. 'I've just got to stop being so proud and hand all my problems over to God.'

It was about an hour after Sheesha had returned home when Beth arrived back. As she pulled the heavy pram into the hall after her, a wave of pure happiness hit her like an atlantic roller. 'Sheesha,' she called eagerly. 'I'll make her a cup of coffee and take it up,' she thought happily. 'I just feel like giving her a huge hug.' As the kettle boiled, Beth remembered with pleasure the happy time she had just spent in the cosy study at the Manse. She and Michael had renewed the marriage vows they had made a year ago, and they had handed over their two children and all the problems that surrounded them to God. 'Something really wonderful happened to me in that study,' thought Beth, as she carried the coffee upstairs. 'God touched me.' The first thing that worried Beth was the silence. No music boomed from Sheesha's bedroom and when she pushed open the door the place looked so tidy it was hard to believe anyone had ever slept there.

'She's not usually this late,' thought Beth feeling slightly deflated. 'Never mind, I'll get on with the supper while Edward is still asleep.' On the way home she had bought steak and mushrooms and she was planning a surprise anniversary meal by candlelight. 'We'll all sit by the fire,' she thought, 'and I'll let them have their classical music on, and they can even read their books.' She was carrying some logs into the lounge when she had the next shock. Someone had lit the lamps and Sheesha's school bag lay on the sofa. 'So she *is* home after all,' thought Beth, fighting a wave of irritation. Then she saw the note. She stood gazing down at it as it lay on the coffee table, and suddenly her arms felt weak with horror and the logs fell onto the rug in a spray of sawdust.

I just can't go on living any longer. You don't want me now you've got Edward. I'm only in the way. School says I can't do medicine so there's no point in life any more. Goodbye. Sheesha.

A feeling of frantic panic seized Beth. This just could not be happening. Not on the very day God had touched her, and let her see Sheesha through His eyes. How could she do it? 'There may still be time if I can find her,' she gasped. Edward was crying again, but for once Beth ignored him as she ran from room to room. As a ward sister in a psychiatric ward she had nursed many attempted suicides and her stomach contracted at the ghastly thought of slashed wrists and hot bathwater. She was so sure the bathroom door was going to be locked that she practically fell into the room and came face to face with the open medicine cupboard.

'Oh, no!' she groaned. 'I knew I should have chucked

those pills out when I first found them, there were enough in there to do the job three times over.'

'Oh, Michael,' she squeaked as she clutched the telephone receiver, 'she must have meant to do it properly. If she'd just wanted to frighten us she'd have stayed here to give us a chance of finding her in time.'

'I'll be right there,' replied Michael, much to the rage of the patient who was in the middle of his tale of woe. 'In the mean time ring the police, and get them to look for her.'

The rain that lashed against the bay windows of the lounge could certainly not be decribed as an April shower. 'She'd hardly go out onto the common in this,' said Michael when he and Beth had searched the coal cellar, outside loo and the garages. 'But I'm going out there anyway,' he added as he hurried to find his wellingtons. The phone startled them both to such an extent they froze like a video that suddenly sticks.

'Could be the police,' muttered Michael and grabbed the phone.

'Oh, Doctor Davidson,' grated the voice of Sister Gertrude. 'I've no doubt you will have heard Meggan's version of the scene at school today, so I feel I must now give you the correct picture.'

'I haven't had a chance to talk to her yet,' snapped Michael, 'but if you have said anything to her that is unjust or untrue, I'm afraid you are going to be very sorry.'

An enraged spluttering noise travelled down the telephone line. 'You must know that your daughter is in serious trouble,' hissed the nun as soon as she could speak.

'Well, I'm very much afraid she has found a way out of it,' said Michael, who was shaking so violently he had to sit down. 'She has disappeared with a pot of sleeping pills and she's left us a suicide note.'

There was a very long silence this time and no more spluttering. 'She was very rude to one of the sisters but I wouldn't have thought that . . .'

'She says in her note that you told her medicine was out of the question,' put in Michael.

'Well, I didn't mean that exactly,' blustered Sister Gertrude as the memory of Sheesha's stricken face returned with sickening force. 'I simply wanted to frighten her into better behaviour.

'Well I don't think any of us have taken the trouble to understand the kid,' said Michael. 'We're all to blame.' And when he had promised to ring the convent later he put down the phone.

After two hours of splashing through the rain and mud on the common he was back in the kitchen trying to force a hot drink down into his heaving stomach. That evening was probably the worst of their lives – two violently active people quite unable to do anything but sit and wait for . . . what?

Then the doorbell rang. Holding hands for support they rushed into the hall.

'It's probably the police,' whispered Michael, 'we've both got to be brave.'

Chapter Twelve

Carefully, Sheesha carried the pot of pills downstairs and when she had collected a can of coke she went into the lounge. She had always loved this room. It would be the perfect place to die.

The fire was grey and dead like her hopes for the future, and ominous dark clouds filled the sky outside. Slowly she walked round the room, lighting the lamps one by one, and watching them illuminate the pictures she loved so much. Then for the last time she put Debussy on the record player and let the piercingly sweet, tragic music reach her soul.

'I must write them a note,' she thought, 'something that'll make them feel guilty.' She pulled a piece of paper from her biology folder and began to write. The result was rather like something from a black and white film, but it suited her mood exactly.

'Now for it!' she thought rather nervously. No sooner did she pick up the pot of pills than she felt her throat closing involuntarily. The mere sight of a pill always did that to her. Once as a tiny child she had choked on a fruit gum and the memory of being held upside down by the feet and banged furiously on the back had lived with her ever since. She could never take a pill now without remembering the panic of that day.

'I'm going to swallow them all!' she told herself firmly, 'and no hassle.' But the first two stuck in her throat despite the coke and she had to spit them out into the wastepaper basket.

'I've got to hurry,' she told herself firmly, 'I'm just going to sit here until the pot's empty,' and curling into an armchair she closed her eyes. How wonderful it was going to be. Just to go to sleep and never wake up again. Then the doorbell rang. Sheesha felt cross, why couldn't people even give you the chance to die in peace. 'I'll keep quiet and they'll think everyone's out,' she thought, as she took another pill, but she forgot the light streaming out into the dark wet afternoon. Suddenly a tall figure appeared at the french window and someone tapped on the glass. Sheesha froze where she sat. The Irishman! The outline looked the same. He had come back to get her at last. Slowly the french door opened, for Beth in her usual disorganised way had gone out without doing up the catches.

'Perhaps he'll kill me straight away and then I won't have to bother with any wretched pills,' she thought almost hopefully.

'I'm looking for Doctor Davidson,' said a pleasant velvety voice without the slightest trace of an Irish accent. 'He said he would met me here.'

As he walked towards her, Sheesha felt as if everything inside her stopped with a jolt. Not only her heart, but the very blood in her veins, even her salivary glands dried up. It was not fear. She could see he was not the Irishman, just the most good-looking boy she had ever encountered in her life. It was his smile that stopped her heartbeat and the way his eyes crinkled at the corners. Both his hands were heavily bandaged and she assumed he was one of her father's patients.

'I know who you are,' he said pleasantly. 'You're the terrible witch of Gravely. I used to be in the year below you, but I remember you well.' How could she have been at the same school as this boy and never noticed him or the way his hair curled into his neck?

'My name's Zac,' he said, sitting down on the arm of the sofa, 'Zac Farroudi, but you're not Mary Jenkins these days are you?'

How she had always despised the cliche 'love at first sight'. This ridiculous thing could not be happening to her. It was purely a chemical reaction.

'I'm Meggan Davidson,' she croaked, and fought a desperate desire to tell this stranger exactly what she intended to do. Instead she put another pill into her mouth only to choke it up again in the same undignified manner.

'You're not having a lot of luck with those pills, are you?' Zac smiled. 'Have you got the flu or something? You certainly look a bit mildewed.'

'Thanks for nothing,' said Sheesha sarcastically, as she tried another pill. 'Actually I'm in the middle of killing myself.' The dramatic effect of the statement was ruined as the pill clung to her throat and she coughed and gagged until her eyes ran. It was hardly the best way to attract a young man, and he obviously thought she was joking, for he laughed heartily as he banged her between the shoulder blades.

'I mean it!' she spluttered crossly, as soon as she could speak. 'These are sleeping pills, I haven't got any down yet but I intend to take the lot.'

She thought he might grab the pot or dash and dial 999, but he just smiled that fatal smile again and said, 'Why?' as if he really wanted to know.

'My life is in ruins,' replied Sheesha tragically, and paused for effect, but all he said was,

'So's mine, but I'm not a coward.'

'Neither am I!' countered Sheesha indignantly. 'It takes a lot of nerve to kill yourself.'

'But it takes an awful lot more to go on living,' he countered. 'Any fool can die, that's easy.'

140

Sheesha scrutinised him through half-closed eyes, analysing every detail of him with her computer-like brain. His clothes looked expensive, he was startlingly good-looking and he had the self assured manner of someone who was always the centre of attraction. How could someone like this possibly feel their life was in ruins?

'You don't know what it's like to be desperate,' she said, taking a tentative sip of coke.

'Well, a couple of months ago, I certainly didn't,' he agreed. 'My father was terribly well-off and he gave me everything I asked him for. Then one night we were raided and he was arrested for running a drugs ring and swindling people on a giant scale.'

'You're Farroudi's son,' gasped Sheesha as she recalled the bombshell that had recently hit Fleetbridge, causing the town to crawl with press men and TV cameras for days. 'You live in that gorgeous house over the common.'

'Lived,' corrected Zac sadly. 'Now Dad's in prison. Everything he owned has gone towards paying his debts. I haven't as much as a two pence piece, and they'll send him down for so long I doubt if he'll live long enough to ever come out. For the first few days I did nothing but plan ways of killing myself.'

'Did you slash your wrists?' asked Sheesha, looking curiously at his bandaged hands.

'Oh, no,' he replied hastily, sinking them into his pockets and looking embarrassed. 'I never got to the point of actually "doing" anything.'

'What stopped you then?' asked Sheesha curiously.

'God I suppose,' replied Zac rather shyly. 'I didn't have anywhere to live, so my friend David took me home to his parents and I've been there ever since. I expect you know them, the Martins, he's a minister.'

'You mean you're living at the Manse, with all that rabble,' said Sheesha incredulously.

'They're not a rabble,' said Zac stiffly, 'they're the nicest people I've ever met.'

'But surely someone like you, with a father like yours, isn't religious?'

'You don't have to be good to ask God into your life,' grinned Zac. 'In fact the worse you are the easier it is to do! Of course I didn't know anything about God until I went to the Martins, but I was so down that Mr Martin asked me to direct a passion play for Easter. I'm into drama, you see. Well, reading all about Jesus and then acting His part in the play, I suddenly realized just how much he went through to make me happy. I feel like new now, just as if I'm starting all over again. Now it's your turn, what ruined your life?'

'He doesn't really care,' Sheesha told herself firmly, 'he's only trying to make you talk, like they do when someone's about to jump off a tower block. He's like all men, he only wants to be a hero. When he's got all the glory for saving your life, he won't want to know you then and you'll be as badly off as ever.'

'Are you still a witch?' he asked, as the silence between them began to feel embarrassing.

'No,' replied Sheesha wearily, 'but I don't want to belong to God either. Why can't we all just be free to run our own show?'

He stood up then, and leant against the mantlepiece, his hands still hidden in his pockets and as he looked down at her she found herself thinking what long eyelashes he had. Something incredibly pleasant was happening inside her school jumper that had never happened in there before!

'I don't think we can ever be free,' he said at last. 'I used to think I was, but then I got hooked on the booze and it got to be my boss in the end. Money ruined my Dad's life, and I've got a friend called Steve, his temper is in charge of him!' Suddenly he removed his hands and smiled down ruefully at them. 'I suppose Mr Martin is about the freest person I know,' he continued, 'and even he's controlled by God. Something or someone always controls us in the end. perhaps we all have to find the best boss to work for.'

Sheesha sat gazing up at this unusual boy. 'He's deep enough for me,' she thought, 'at last I've found a man who doesn't bore me. if the world contains someone like this, why do I want to leave it?'

'Mr Martin is a very sensible sort of a man,' said Zac. 'Why don't you talk to him before you kill youself the next time?' He put his head on one side and smiled again, and Sheesha was lost – lost for life, and she knew it.

'How many of these things have you managed to swallow?' he continued.

'None,' she admitted.

'Then will you let me have them – just for safety?'

'Why should I?' challenged Sheesha.

'Because I think I'd mind very much if you weren't around any more. Most girls bore me, but you're different.' Sheesha could have sworn she heard violins playing in the distance.

'Come on home and have tea,' he suggested. 'I don't want to leave you here all alone, and it doesn't look as if your father is going to show. But you'll have to put up with the rabble,' he finished with another of his devastating smiles.

'But don't you want to see Dad about your hands?' asked Sheesha.

'Oh, no,' he replied suddenly looking embarrassed again, 'they're nearly better, I just had a message for him from Mr Martin.'

'What's the matter with your hands?' demanded Sheesha. The doctor in her could never pass anyone with so much as a plaster sticking to them without wanting to know how they hurt themselves and what treatment they were receiving.

'You ought to fasten those french doors,' he said, firmly changing the subject. 'You don't want any more burglars breaking in, do you?'

Sheesha, who was in the habit of imposing her will on everyone around her, found herself following this extraordinary person meekly and silently from the house, and as she walked with him across Fleetbridge she was conscious that her life would never be the same again.

'But whatever went wrong?' demanded Sheesha as she sat on the shabby leather sofa where her father and Beth had sat only a short while before. Something quite monumental was happening to Sheesha. For sixteen years she had carefully dammed up all her feelings in a great deep reservoir far down inside herself and only ever allowed herself to communicate with anyone on a purely surface level. But the compelling eyes of the insignificant looking little Minister felt like two sticks of dynamite blasting their way through her carefully constructed dam. She had been talking to him for more than two hours and the pressure that had built up inside her head and reached an unbearable level was now seeping away.

'He really wants to know,' she thought, 'and he understands exactly what I'm saying.'

'When I came into church that day, I really wanted to give myself to God. I didn't want to go on being empty like that cottage I told you about. But just as I began to pray I felt this terrible choking feeling, and I panicked. I felt such a fool behaving like that. I'll never be able to come to church again.'

'Well, of course that is just what Satan wants,' smiled Mr Martin.

'Dad said because I'd been so useful to Satan he was

fighting hard not to let me go,' continued Sheesha. 'Does that mean I can never get away?'

'That's just another lie Satan's been telling you,' replied the Minister. 'Jesus actually gave us complete authority over Satan and in the name of Jesus we could tell him to "shove off" right now. But you are never going to be safe while you stand empty like the cottage. You must open up all your doors and windows and let God pour in.'

'But even if I do that, I won't be all that different,' said Sheesha cautiously, 'Dad and Beth aren't saints.'

'Neither am I,' laughed Mr Martin. 'This process of being filled up with God takes all our lives. There has to be a point when we first open the door to Him, but when He steps in He finds us full of all kinds of rubbish and unpleasant mess. Resentments, wrong attitudes, habits, you name it, He'll find it. If He cleared them all away at once it would blow our minds, but He gently points them out to us one by one, and helps us to get rid of them, and of course the more we chuck out the more room we leave inside ourselves for God and all the lovely positive things He brings with Him.'

'Well, if it's going to take all my life, let's get started right now,' said Sheesha with a shudder. 'I'm so frightened something might go wrong.'

As she knelt next to Mr Martin, Sheesha could feel her heart crashing itself painfully against her ribs, as she waited for the ice cold hands to close round her neck, but instead of fear she experienced nothing but a huge warm wave of happiness.

'In the name of Jesus,' said Mr Martin, 'you are to leave Meggan alone. We forbid you to frighten her or speak into her mind. Go now, and never come back.' Tears of relief trickled down Sheesha's thin cheeks and then Mr Martin said, 'You talk to God now, and just ask him in.' She felt she actually had a door key in her hand and she found herself lifting it up as if she was presenting it to someone on a great throne.

'Please come in,' she whispered, 'you'll find lots of mess, so please help to clear it up.' Suddenly she opened her eyes and said, 'Could I ask Him to help me become a doctor?'

'You've just made Him the boss, He may not want you to be a doctor.' Sheesha jumped to her feet indignantly. 'You mean I just handed myself over to a God who can't even answer my prayers!'

'But you haven't handed yourself over to Him unless you can trust Him to do what is really best for you.'

Sheesha sat gazing into the fire for a long time, and then slowly she slid back onto her knees.

'Alright, God. No more conditions, do it your way.'

'I'm terribly good at fouling things up,' she said as they both stood up some minutes later. 'Will He leave me if I do?'

'No, He'll never leave you, but you have to keep those windows and doors open to allow more and more of him to come in all the time.'

'I don't really understand you,' said Sheesha nervously.

'Well, we let God into our lives through reading the Bible, praying, coming to church and spending time with other Christians. Telling other people what has happened to you is very important too. Come on, let's make a start on that now.'

As usual the Manse kitchen was crowded with people; supper had been over for hours, but they were still sitting round the table drinking coffee when Sheesha and Mr Martin walked in. Their faces merged into each other in a smiling blur, but Sheesha sensed Carolyn was there and she distinctly saw David Martin holding hands with Manda, but there was really only one person she wanted to see in sharp focus.

146

'Tell them what's just happened,' smiled Mr Martin, and Sheesha felt as if someone had thrown her into the deep end of the swimming pool. Manda and Carolyn were both hugging her long before she had stammered through more than a sentence, and Zac smiled at her until nightingales sang in her ears.

'How wonderful just to be alive!' she thought as happiness surrounded her like a cosy warm duvet. 'I would have been dead by now if it had not been for Zac.'

'You look as if you haven't eaten in months,' said Mrs Martin kindly, as she produced a huge plate of cheese sandwiches, and suddenly Sheesha felt incredibly hungry.

'She'll have to be in your drama group, Zac,' she heard Manda say. 'He's started a drama group, Sheesha,' she explained. 'We've done some one act plays in church as part of the services, and now we've got bookings with other churches too. You should see her act, Zac,' she added enthusiastically. 'You're brilliant, but she's even better!'

Zac looked up with sudden interest. 'We do badly need another girl,' he said, 'but mostly they're too inhibited to let themselves get into their parts.'

As she looked at him across the table, she knew that the one thing she now wanted was to gain this boy's interest and approval. 'Give me an audition now,' she said, springing to her feet. 'Guess who this is.' No one who had ever been to Gravely School could possibly have failed to recognise Mr Atkins the Headmaster. There he stood, taking school assembly, peering over his glasses with his thumbs tucked into his waistcoat. 'I'm waiting for complete silence,' came the familiar pompous voice, followed by the little nervous cough and then the crack of his finger joints as he snapped them. Zac shouted with laughter, and applauded loudly. 'Brilliant, brilliant! You're in. Now give us Mr Saxby the caretaker.'

If Beth and Michael, sitting tensely by their phone, could have seen into the Manse kitchen at that moment, they would have been incredibly surprised. When the doorbell finally rang at ten thirty they were startled to find, not the police or an ambulance but a crowd of young people, talking and laughing loudly and looking as if they had just come from a party. Dumb with astonishment they stood gazing as Sheesha pushed past them and ran up the stairs.

'This is too much,' snorted Beth. 'Go home, the lot of you,' and she slammed the door.

'Oh, you shouldn't have sent them away,' complained Sheesha as she reappeared. 'I wanted Zac to fasten this for me. But will you do it instead, Dad?' With his brain reeling from the shock Michael fastened the silver chain around Sheesha's neck. 'There now,' she smiled, 'I'm wearing God's sign now, because I really belong to Him.'

'But the note . . . the sleeping pills,' faltered Michael. 'We thought . . .'

'The note!' gasped Sheesha in horror. 'I forgot to remove it. I'm sorry. Zac rescued me and took me off to the the Manse to find God.'

Suddenly Beth began to laugh. Michael's strained face relaxed and he joined in. Sheesha looked at them both in mingled exasperation and wonder, then suddenly she began to laugh too, and soon they were making so much noise the worst happened. Edward woke up!

Chapter Thirteen

'How dare you talk to me like that!' screamed Sheesha, her voice rising shrill and spiteful. 'I'll teach you to start preaching at me!' And picking up the rolling pin from the table she began to hit Zac with all her strength.

'Cut! Cut!' he shouted in protest. 'The trouble with you, Sheesha, is you're too good at acting,' he added, rubbing his shoulder ruefully. 'You get so deep into the part, you become it.'

'Sorry,' laughed Sheesha, 'but it won't look realistic unless I actually hit you.'

'You'll break my arm before we perform this play on Sunday morning!' argued Zac.

'Let's have a break,' suggested Manda, 'and go to the chippy for some coke!' The church hall was sweltering hot even at ten o'clock at night, and the May heatwave made them all feel they were in an airless oven.

'It's taking shape at last,' said Zac, rubbing his sweating face with a towel, 'but we'll have to run through it a couple of times more after the break.' The play that Zac had dashed off in the back of a chemistry lesson was a brilliantly perceptive piece of writing, focusing on the difficulties encountered by a boy when he tells his family and then his school friends that he has become a Christian. Sheesha played his sarcastic and bad-tempered mother, and Zac had been right when he said she had become the part.

'Blood, sweat, toil and tears!' muttered Manda, as they went to the chip shop. 'He always was a slave driver.'

'All the best producers are,' replied Sheesha indignantly. 'He's magnificent.'

It was still incredibly hot when they flopped down on the grass that surrounded the church buildings with their cans and greasy packets of chips. Sheesha sat leaning her back against the trunk of a cherry tree, tucking into her chips without even feeling guilty.

How extraordinary that life could change so completely in only one month. She had felt so isolated all her life, and now suddenly she was surrounded by hoards of people who really seemed to care for her. The Manse had become her second home, not that she wanted to escape from her first home now. All the hate she had once held for Beth was gone and school was going well too. Michael had actually neglected his morning surgery to take Sheesha to the Sacred Heart the morning after her row with Sister Gertrude, and he soon had the two nuns charmed and mollified. Sheesha had astonished herself by the magnificence of the apology she thought she would never be able to make to Sister Barbara.

'This religious conversion that you say occurred last night,' Sister Gertrude had said, 'if as the term goes on, we see it making a real difference to your attitude to other members of the school and if it gives you a more balanced outlook on life, then I see no reason why we should not put you forward as an Oxbridge candidate.'

'Nothing's going to go wrong now,' whispered Sheesha happily as she munched a chip. 'I really would be living happily ever after if only . . .' Her eyes travelled towards Zac. As usual he was in the centre of a noisy group of admirers. David was always saying Zac attracted people towards him as if he had swallowed a magnet. 'I'm just one of a whole crowd of people to him,' thought Sheesha.

'He's nice to me, but then he's nice to everyone else as well.' A sudden spurt of anger shot through her. She had always said she would never allow herself to be dependent on any man like this. The happiness of her whole day depended on a smile from Zac, or whether she managed to sit next to him in church, or at the Manse kitchen table. 'I want him all to myself,' she thought, 'but how can I make him notice me?' Now she was gaining weight she had lost that brittle spidery look, but she wished she could cut off her legs at the knee.

'He's so different and so special,' she thought tenderly as a tear trickled down the side of her face.

She shut her eyes so she could picture again that first Sunday after she had given herself to God. She had sat in church at the end of a row next to Manda. Halfway through the first hymn Zac had come in late and the sidesman had placed a chair in the aisle for him next to hers. She had never sat this close to a boy before in her life. He smelt of exotic aftershave and she could not listen to a word of the sermon as she fought the delicious stabbing pain in her stomach. 'There's a simple chemical and biological explanation for this,' she told herself furiously, but nevertheless, she liked it. But why was he wearing gloves? His hands were not bandaged anymore, so was he trying to hide some kind of skin disease? When they reached the last hymn the collection plate appeared and Zac fumbled in his jacket pocket. It is difficult to find a coin in thick leather gloves.

'I'm sorry,' he muttered to the waiting sidesman, and was at last forced to pull off his glove. As he put his ten pence piece in the plate Sheesha froze with horror. What on earth could have caused such an injury? Without thinking she took his hand and turned it over, then she ripped off his other glove and sat gazing at his distorted hands as she held them in her own.

'Who did that to you?' she gasped as the congregation sang lustily all around them. To her great embarrassment she found she was crying so much that her tears fell onto his hands and he put his arm around her and gently led her from the church.

'Don't get so steamed up,' he said awkwardly. 'I thought you said you were going to be a doctor.'

'Someone rammed some kind of stake right through your hands,' said Sheesha. 'They smashed the bones and then you must have hung by them to cause that much distortion.'

'Sherlock Holmes couldn't have done better,' he laughed. 'You're a genius.'

'But why? And who did it?' demanded Sheesha, as Zac pulled his gloves back on.

'When I told my mates I'd become a Christian it riled them a bit, and they decided to crucify me too.' Zac smiled. 'If Manda and the rest of the group hadn't rescued me it might have been a bit nasty, but as it was, it taught me a lot.'

'Taught you what?' gasped Sheesha.

'How he felt when they did it to Him. It made me sure I'd done the right thing in giving myself over to Him!'

'You really love God enough to let people do that to you?' said Sheesha incredulously.

'Well, He loved me that much,' he replied simply. 'But actually I didn't have much choice at the time.'

People were streaming out of the church now and they were surrounded like a sandcastle submerged by the incoming tide.

'I hope I'll get to love Him that much too,' whispered Sheesha and she turned to run all the way home.

That had been the only time she had really talked to Zac on his own and suddenly she found herself aching for him.

'Come on you lazy lot,' called the voice she heard so

often in her dreams, 'back to work, and Pam, try not to giggle this time. And if you hit me with that rolling pin Sheesha, so help me, I'll find myself another mother!'

'Yes, life was fun,' thought Sheesha, 'and it was wonderfully good to be alive.'

When she went home that night Sheesha crept into the nursery and stood looking down at Edward. Beth had finally got him to sleep by rocking the cot and now she seemed afraid to stop. His cheeks were scarlet with health and over-exercised lungs, and his hair stuck up in damp spikes.

'He's growing up,' thought Sheesha heavily. 'He looks more like a boy than a baby now.' She glanced up at Beth and whispered, 'You look tired out.' Beth smiled back through the shadows, pleased she had noticed.

'It's your birthday tomorrow, isn't it? Why don't you go out to dinner with Dad, and let me babysit? After all I ruined your wedding anniversary.'

'That's a fine suggetion,' came another whisper from the door, and there stood Michael, with his glasses pushed up to the top of his head.

'Oh, I don't know,' hesitated Beth. 'I've never left him before.'

'Don't you trust me?' demanded Sheesha with a sudden edge to her whisper. Deep down Beth did not trust her. Edward was the greatest achievement of her life, and the thought of handing him over to someone she knew didn't like him worried her.

'Come on Beth,' pleaded Michael. 'You mustn't let yourself get obsessive over him you know.'

'I don't think I should leave him,' said Beth uneasily.

'Right then!' snorted Sheesha with a sudden return of her old anger. 'I won't offer again,' and she stomped off into her room and slammed the door with such force that Edward woke up and bawled for three long exhausing hours.

'I thought I wouldn't feel like that now,' thought Sheesha as she sat at her window watching the common turn to silver in the moonlight. There was no point in lying in bed trying to sleep with that noise going on next door.

'She doesn't really trust me – *she* hasn't really changed either.

The same old anger flared up again and it frightened Sheesha. 'This process of being filled up with God takes a lifetime,' said Mr Martin out of the shadows of her memory.

'Sorry God,' muttered Sheesha, 'here's a bit more rubbish for you.'

In the next room Beth was suffering from much the same kind of misery as she paced up and down the room with Edward in her arms. 'It was my fault she was upset tonight,' she thought. 'I must show her I love and trust her now – however difficult it is.'

They all groped their way to the kitchen next morning rather bleary-eyed and short of asleep.

'I'm sorry,' said Beth and Sheesha both at exactly the same time, and they burst out laughing.

'I'm more sorry than either of you,' yawned Michael. 'I seriously considered giving Edward an injection of morphine to shut him up in the end!'

Sheesha could never recall ever giving anyone a birthday present before, but she produced one now, and laid it shyly on the table.

'Happy birthday,' she muttered.

'How lovely!' exclaimed Beth when she opened the parcel and discovered a bone china mug. 'You couldn't have given me anything better. Thank you, love!'

'I promise never to throw it at you,' said Sheesha as she experienced the unusual sensation of laughter bubbling up inside her. At the sight of Michael's bewildered expression, Beth burst out laughing too, and hugged Sheesha impulsively.

'What's the joke?' demanded Michael as he shook the infuriating toaster that had stuck once again.

'Let me babysit for you tonight,' pleaded Sheesha, partly to change the subject. Beth hesitated with her hand held out towards the milk bottle. She could see this really mattered to Sheesha, so she fought down the desire to suggest that Manda or Carolyn come over to give her a hand and forced herself to smile.

'Thanks love,' she said, 'we'll take you up on that.'

Looking back on that day it seemed to Sheesha as if every detail was engraved on her mind like a diamond cutting a pattern on glass.

She remembered sneaking into the school library and looking out a book on child care. She only wanted a diagram on how to change a nappy, but she read the whole book before she realised she was missing Physics. All the same she felt she knew everything there was to know about the management of babies now, and went home quite looking forward to the evening.

Edward knew perfectly well they were going out, and he took so long over his bottle that Michael nearly exploded.

'Let Sheesha give him the rest,' he said, 'we've booked the table for eight, we're going to be late as it is.'

'But you must make sure he burps,' insisted Beth anxiously, 'and put him down on his tummy in case he's sick.'

'For goodness sake!' protested Sheesha. 'I know what to do, I've read a book on it.'

'Some books say you must leave babies to cry,' fussed Beth, 'you won't do that, will you?'

'If he cries, I'll put my pillow over his head and sit on it,' threatened Sheesha. It was only a joke, but Sheesha spent the rest of her life regretting those careless words.

Chapter Fourteen

'I don't like you, Edward,' said Sheesha as she heard the car slide away over the gravel. 'So you'd better behave.' Edward spat the teat out of his mouth and looked up at her intensely then suddenly from deep inside his tummy a strange rumbling noise began, it bubbled up to his throat and caused his mouth to split into a huge grin. 'You're laughing,' exclaimed Sheesha. 'I didn't know you could do that. What a lovely noise!' How she despised people who make ridiculous noises to babies, but suddenly there she was doing the same, while her small brother's body convulsed itself with amusement. 'You and I might have a lot of fun one day,' whispered Sheesha. 'Perhaps you're not so bad after all.'

The laughter seemed to give Edward an appetite and he soon began to suck his bottle with miraculous rapidity. He then burped with vulgar abandonment, and fell fast asleep on Sheesha's lap.

A vast sense of achievement flooded her as she laid him in his cot, and then went down to wash the bottle. 'I might even get that essay done after all,' she thought happily.

While she waited for the kettle to boil for a cup of coffee, she picked up Beth's nursing magazine that lay among the debris on the table. As she flipped idly through it the title of one article made her freeze.

Cot Death, The Unexplained Tragedy

Slowly she sat down at the table and began to read with her usual astounding speed.

'In spite of extensive research,' concluded the last paragraph, 'there still seems no reason why some babies are found dead in their cots each morning. The tragic fact remains that certain babies simply stop breathing.'

Leaving the kettle to boil angrily, Sheesha dashed upstairs and burst into the nursery. Edward was positively snoring, and feeling like an overanxious mother hen she crept away.

She was just settling down at her desk when the doorbell rang. She ignored it at first, after all it would only be a patient wanting something ridiculous like pills for constipation, but when it rang again she shot up from her chair in horror. Suppose it woke Edward! 'There's never any peace in this house,' she muttered as she ran down the stairs, 'nothing but phones and doorbells, but I suppose that's the price you pay for being a doctor.'

Still feeling cross she opened the door a suspicious inch and looked out into the dusk. So when a velvety voice said, 'Hi there,' she was completely unprepared for the hurricane of joy that hit her.

'I'm afraid Dad's not in,' she gasped.

'No matter,' said Zac pleasantly but he did not turn away.

'I've just boiled the kettle,' said Sheesha in her shy jerky way. 'Would you like a coffee?' Suddenly it mattered to her more than anything else in the world that he stayed.

'Thanks,' he grinned, stepping into the hall. 'It'll be nice to drink one in peace away from the "rabble".'

'Well it's not often peaceful here,' said Sheesha, 'but the monster's asleep for once. I'm babysitting tonight, and if he wakes up now I'll kill him.'

'Your parents must be crazy,' laughed Zac. 'I wouldn't trust you to sit a goldfish.'

'Why?' demanded Sheesha, quite nettled.

'Well, you're not the motherly type are you?'

They carried their coffee mugs into the lounge and Sheesha lit the lamps and opened the french doors. 'It's lovely sitting here looking out over the common when it's getting dark,' she said dreamily. 'Shall I put a record on? What kind of music do you like?'

'Pop,' he smiled. 'Heavy rock really.'

'We've only got classical stuff,' apologised Sheesha, feeling suddenly sad.

'Put on something you like, then,' he said softly. 'You never know, you might convert me.'

'Last time you came here you converted me,' commented Sheesha as she found her favourite Debussy. Zac laughed again, and she wondered if there was any sound more lovely in the world.

They sat on either end of the velvety sofa that had once filled Beth's dreams and an embarrassed silence settled on them. Suddenly it mattered intensely to Sheesha to know if he had come to see her of whether he was just passing the time because her father was out.

'Why did you come?' she asked rather stiffly.

'That's just what I like about you,' chuckled Zac. 'You never waste time babbling or chattering, you just say what you're thinking, straight out.'

'But why?' continued Sheesha firmly.

'Well, I suppose I'd better not babble or chatter either,' he said softly. 'I actually came to see you. There's something on my mind, and I thought you'd be the only person who would actually understand how I feel.' He stopped suddenly, searching for his usual self assurance that for once seemed to have trickled away from him. 'You're not like anyone else I've ever met,' he continued awkwardly. 'You're the most different person I've ever come across. I thought that the moment I broke in through those doors and you were sat there, struggling with those pills.' He put out his hand, in an almost instinctive, absent minded way and touched her hair, followed the line of its kinks and swirls with his finger. 'You've changed so very much since then, you look so . . . different now.' Suddenly he seemed to realize what he was doing and he snatched his hand away and stuffed in into his jacket pocket. 'Sorry,' he muttered. 'Manda told me you're a man-hater. I bet you feel like slapping my face.' Actually no thought was further from Sheesha's mind, but at that moment she could willingly have slapped Manda's. She could not help feeling glad she was sitting down or she might have fallen in a sweaty heap at his feet, but mentally she picked herself up, dusted herself down and carried on with her inquiries.

'What is worrying you?' she asked in a slightly husky voice.

'Well, Manda told me you didn't get on too well with her Aunt Beth until you became a Christian, and you're always saying how much you hate that baby brother of yours, so . . . well, you see, I've got the same problem.'

'But I thought you only had your Dad,' replied Sheesha blankly.

'Well, actually, I've got a mother and a twin brother,' admitted Zac, 'and I've got to leave the Manse and go to live with them.'

Sheesha felt her dream castles falling down round her yet again and she said, 'I suppose they live in Australia.'

'Oh, it's not that bad,' replied Zac with a sudden shadow of his usual smile, 'they live in Fleetbridge, but I just can't stand either of them.'

'I thought twins were supposed to be very close,' frowned Sheesha.

Zac loosened the red silk scarf he was wearing round his neck and cleared his throat awkwardly. 'My brother is a spastic,' he said. 'He's terribly disabled and he can't do anything but sit in his wheelchair wailing and dribbling all over the place.'

'He makes you feel guilty because you're normal,' stated Sheesha.

'Yes,' replied Zac sounding really impressed, 'that's it exactly, how clever you are. Mum's always doted on him and she really excluded me and Dad completely. Dad got sick of it and practically booted them both out, and he and I got stuck together. I just can't forgive her for not giving me a fair share. She almost seemed to blame me for Kevin's handicap. But I've seen what God did for you in only a month, and I wondered if you could help me.'

'Something very wonderful happened to me tonight,' Sheesha said softly. 'I was giving Edward his bottle. I really have hated him, because I thought Dad and Beth would love him instead of me, but last Sunday in church I really asked God to help me love him, and suddenly I really did. He looked up at me and laughed, and I felt he was saying, let's be friends.'

'Will you pray I'll be like that with Kevin and Mum?' asked Zac wistfully. 'I've got to move in with them this week.'

In the Manse it was the fashion to stop and pray on the spot about anything that was worrying anyone, and they usually held hands as they prayed. So Sheesha simply did the same without giving it a second thought. She slid along the sofa, took Zac's hands in hers and began to talk to God without the slightest embarrassment.

'Thank you God,' she began, 'that Zac saved my life in here and dragged me off to Mr Martin so I could find you. Thank you that you took away my hate and put love in me instead. If you can do that for me, you can do it for Zac, so please do. Amen.'

When she had finished they both sat motionless in the

dim light but when Sheesha suddenly realized she was still holding Zac's hands and tried to pull them away, she discovered it was his hands that held hers. Slowly they lifted their eyes and looked at one another. Every girl in the youth group was after this boy – yet he was looking at her – Sheesha, of all people – she could hardly believe it wasn't just another daydream.

'I longed to do this, ever since last night when I saw you sitting under that cherry tree,' he whispered. 'I never thought anyone would ever want to hold my hand ever again, not now they're all smashed up.'

Very slowly and gently Sheesha lifted his hands and kissed the two horrible scars. 'I'm very proud to,' she breathed. Then the phone rang. The fairytale dream world was shattered but the thought of Edward upstairs caused Sheesha to leap to its shrill demands.

It was Manda, and Sheesha had never been less pleased to hear her voice. 'Is Zac there, by any chance?' she asked. 'His Mum's just popped in and wants to see him. She says its urgent.'

'Can I . . . would you mind if I come . . . another time?' asked Zac shyly, as she opened the front door for him. 'I've got my exams coming up soon, and Manda says you're terribly good at explaining things. Would you help me?' Sheesha couldn't think of anything she would rather do, and as she watched him shambling down the drive she found she was shaking all over her body.

She resisted the strong temptation to look in and see if Edward was still breathing, and telling herself not to fuss she sat down to write her essay, and as usual she was soon deeply engrossed. The numbers on her digital clock flashed past unheeded and she did not hear the chimes of the Parish Church clock. She never knew what made her put down her pen so suddenly. All she could remember was an unexpected surge of anxiety. 'I should never have read that silly article,' she muttered as she hurried towards the nursery. 'I'm only panicking because he isn't actually crying for once.' As she opened the nursery door the landing light streamed in through the bars of the cot, and Sheesha knew Edward was dead, and as she stood by the door she felt everything inside her skin slide down onto the floor. The silence was uncanny, and the little bump under the blue blanket looked so oddly flat and still. The scarlet cheeks were gone, and as she snapped on the light she noticed how pale and waxy the little face had become, and how very old.

'I always wanted you to die,' she thought as she stood looking down into the cot, 'until tonight.' As usual the doctor inside her elbowed its way to the front of her mind, and shouted 'Resuscitation – you've got four minutes to play with.' Without a second thought, Sheesha leapt into action. Edward felt like an old-fashioned rag doll as she grabbed him and began to strip off his sleeping suit. 'I must make him gasp,' Sheesha told herself, 'force him to get going.' She banged his back, slapped his legs and the soles of his feet, but deep inside her brain something kept shouting, 'He's too cold, he's been dead much longer than four minutes.'

'*No!*' shouted Sheesha and threw him down on the table. Tipping back his head she put her mouth over his tiny nose and mouth. 'Don't breathe too hard,' she warned herself. 'He's only got tiny lungs.' As she worked following the routine she had learnt so well, little scenes from her past flashed into her mind like clips lifted from a feature film. She saw herself beating her fists against a rock in Ireland. 'I want it to die,' she was screaming to the voice inside her head which replied, 'If you want it dead hard enough it will die!' Then she was walking down the path by the river with Mark. 'Do you think it's possible to kill someone by hate?' she had asked. Well, was it possible – had she killed Edward by some inexplicable force? She had always hated the people around her and all her life she had brought disaster to them wherever she went. Now she seemed to have done so again.

'This can't be happening!' she thought. 'You must breathe, or they'll all think I killed you,' and her own words came back to mock her. 'I'll put a pillow over his head . . .' 'That's what they'll think I did,' she sobbed. The article she had read downstairs in the kitchen had said that no one could ever prove that . . . She must get a doctor, there must be something someone could do. She ran into her parents bedroom and there by the phone lay the number of the Fleetbridge Hotel – Beth was strangely efficient in some things. Michael was only two minutes away, it would certainly be quicker to reach him than one of his partners or an ambulance. But what was Beth going to say? The horror of that was too great for Sheesha, but time was running out.

'Fleetbridge Hotel, can I help you?' said a pleasant voice in her ear that made her jump.

'You have a Doctor Davidson eating in your restaurant,' began Sheesha trying to keep her voice below the pitch of hysteria. 'Can you tell him to come home immediately, it's an emergency.'

'Couldn't they finish their meal first?' asked the receptionist.

'It's a matter of life and death,' shouted Sheesha, and then she knew without doubt that she should have left the word 'life' right out of it.

'What have you done to him?' screamed Beth as a few minutes later she burst through the door. Michael lifted Edward out of Sheesha's arms and laid him in his cot. 'I tried to resuscitate him,' said Sheesha and felt her voice was coming from a long way away. 'I tried everything.'

'You were too late,' said Michael gently. 'He's been gone at least an hour.'

'What were you doing?' screamed Beth. 'Why didn't you watch him?'

'I'll have to ring Jim,' said Michael. 'We'll have to have another doctor to sign the certificate, and we'll have to call the police.'

'Police!' screamed Sheesha. 'You think I killed him then?'

'They always have to come for a cot death,' said Michael wearily, and stumbled away towards the phone.

Time means nothing in a nightmare, and it meant nothing that night. Sheesha sat in the chair in the nursery and watched people move around her like characters in a play. Beth was oddly silent, Michael took refuge behind his professional cloak, while his partner was actually tearful. Suddenly an officious and rather unpleasant voice cut through Sheesha's deathly lethargy.

'I need to ask you some questions young lady.' A young police constable was bending over her, with a notebook in his hand. 'Why did you take off the baby's pyjamas?'

Suddenly Beth's silence broke like a shattered pane of glass and words came crashing through the fragments.

'She said she would put a pillow over his head, constable. I've seen the way she looked at him, she's unstable and dangerous. He probably cried and she lost her temper and started hitting him.'

'Beth!' pleaded Michael. 'You can't accuse someone of murder.'

'All that will show up in the postmortem, Mam,' said the constable grimly.

'Not if she put a pillow over his face,' sobbed Beth.

'I want your story now, and I want the truth,' said the constable, taking Sheesha by the arm. 'Perhaps you'll come and show me what you were doing all the evening.

Two hours later she crept into bed. Every time she shut her eyes she could still see the hard eyes of the constable piercing her and hear his grating voice. The memory of her father's silent reproof bit into her like acid and down the landing Beth was still sobbing, but Sheesha knew that she was far beyond the comfort of tears. Her father had not said one word to her, and Beth had said too many.

'Don't go to school tomorrow, my senior officer will want to see you,' the constable had threatened when he had filled his notebook with her jumbled, incoherent story.

'It always happens,' thought Sheesha as she put her head under her pillow. 'Just when I think life is getting nice, everything always goes wrong.'

'This time it's different,' came a whisper deep down inside her, 'you've got God this time.'

'Mr Martin said God would never desert me, even if I blew it,' she thought, so she slid out from under the duvet and knelt down by the bed. 'Oh, God,' she said in a dry grating whisper. 'I'm so sorry if I killed him because I hated him so much. But you were there when he laughed at me – you know I wasn't hating him then. Please don't leave me now.' And feeling strangely comforted she was soon asleep.

Chapter Fifteen

It was about ten o'clock the next morning when she heard Michael's voice outside her door. She had been dressed for hours, just sitting staring out across the common.

'Do you want some coffee?' he asked, his voice sounding strained and croaky.

'No,' she replied flatly. He turned the door handle but she had taken the precaution of locking it. Desperately she longed for him to batter the door down, rush in and tell her he still loved her, but he simply walked away and his footsteps sounded like those of an old man.

'It's the police, they want to talk to you.' Was she hearing right? That was Mark's voice outside her door. Eagerly she undid the bolt, but the look on Mark's face reminded her of his expression the night Manda had been injured, and Sheesha shrank away from him as if he had hit her.

'I was staying with Mum and Dad. We drove straight here when we heard,' he said coldly.

At the bottom of the stairs stood Manda's mother with her arm round her sister Beth, and it took all Sheesha's courage to walk down the stairs towards her.

'How could you have left that girl in charge of the baby, Beth?' she demanded. 'She's insane, that's what she is.' Sheesha noticed the look that passed between the constable and his sergeant and she felt cold all over.

'If I'd gone in a bit earlier and managed to resuscitate

him, you'd all be thinking I was a hero,' sobbed Sheesha, as she sat alone in the dining room facing the two policemen.

'But you didn't resuscitate him, did you Miss Davidson?' snarled the police sergeant. 'What time did you go in and put the pillow over his face?'

'I didn't,' protested Sheesha. 'You're just trying to muddle me.'

'Your stepmother's sister told us just now that you've already been in trouble with us before,' continued her interrogator, 'sent to Parkfield weren't you? Now, let's go back over your story again. I put it to you that when your boyfriend came round you were having such fun you wanted to keep the baby quiet at all costs. You didn't want him disturbing you, did you?'

'He's not my boyfriend,' snarled Sheesha, and you can ask him, he knows Edward didn't wake up while he was here.'

'We have asked him,' put in the constable, 'but with a father like his, quite frankly we wouldn't believe a word he says.' For what seemed like hours they questioned and re-questioned Sheesha, cornering her, tripping her up and goading her into a state of stupidity.

'If you go on changing your story like this,' smiled the objectionable Sergeant, 'it will only make things worse for you. We will have to come back every day to question you until the results of the postmortem come in so you had better stay indoors, and do some serious thinking.'

When they had gone Sheesha staggered into the kitchen in search of coffee. But Mark and his parents stood between her and the kettle and they felt like a solid wall of dislike and disapproval. Her father and Beth sat at the table and they looked up at her with eyes that did not see. She felt they looked through her, as if she had ceased to exist as surely as little Edward. She had no family really, she had been a fool to think she had, and turning she ran back to the safety of her room. Had she known a little more about people she would have realized that her father and Beth had not really seen her. They were suffering from shock and profound grief, they were not rejecting her, she simply did not exist for them at that moment.

Mark did not hate her, but he had never been able to understand her and that worried him. Girls to him were straightforward objects to be used for one purpose only. Sheesha did not fit into that mould so she baffled him. Mrs Williams had loved her once and been bitterly hurt by her. She did not know God, and had allowed hate and bitterness to rule her ever since Manda's accident; and Mr. Williams never had any thought or emotion of his own, he simply took his colour from his wife like a chameleon. But to Sheesha, weak from shock and lack of food, they all seemed to have turned against her.

'That girl has caused us all nothing but misery,' came Mrs Williams' voice from the landing outside. 'She's repaid all our kindness by nothing short of treachery.' She was obviously escorting Beth up to her room to lie down, but her words stuck in Sheesha's confused mind like a cracked gramophone record. She was desperately hungry, but no one called her down to a meal. She thought it was because they wanted her to starve. Actually it was because it never occurred to any of them to eat that day except Mark, who went off to the pub and ate an enormous meal as usual.

It was about seven o'clock when she seemed to have reached her lowest point. She had dropped off into a shallow sleep and dreamed she was being dragged back to Parkfield. As the familiar smell of the dreadful place engulfed her she woke screaming and fighting frantically with her duvet. 'Not that, God,' she sobbed. 'Don't let them take me away. If you still love me and you still want

168

to live inside me, then let someone from the Manse come round and see me.' She felt so sure God would answer her prayer that she got up, washed, did her hair and sat down by the window to watch. Would it be Mr Martin, or would it be Manda? Suddenly she saw a figure coming across the common, stumbling along with long loose strides. It could only be one person. 'Zac!' she breathed. 'Oh God, you sent Zac, I didn't dare to ask you for a miracle that big.' As he approached the gate, Zac tightened his pace to a slow funeral tread, and as he stepped into the drive he stopped altogether. He was obviously feeling embarrassed and not at all sure of his reception. Had those ghastly policemen been mean to him too, she wondered, made him feel like a criminal as well? Suddenly another figure appeared from the road on the right, running quickly towards Zac on ridiculous high heels. 'Carolyn,' gasped Sheesha, 'what's she saying to him?' There she stood, perfect in every detail like a fragile china doll, looking adoringly up at him. What man can resist that kind of perfection? 'That used to be my best friend,' thought Sheesha as she saw Carolyn slip her arm through Zac's and lead him away up the road.

'That's it then, isn't it,' sobbed Sheesha. 'God doesn't love me anymore – and I've even lost Zac. She was probably telling him he didn't want to go near a mentally unbalanced murderer. She knows all the things I used to say about Edward, and she'll tell him the lot.' 'I wouldn't trust you to babysit a goldfish.' His remembered words felt like the contents of a hoover bag in her throat.

Slowly and wearily she took a bag from the bottom of her wardrobe and started to stuff it full of miscellaneous clothes. She found five pounds in her bag and a bar of chocolate. 'Survival rations,' she thought grimly and ate it all without tasting a bite. When she had zipped up her cagoule she sat down again at the window to wait for dusk.

This was the only way. She could not stay here to be rejected and hated, then finally locked up as insane. There was no past, no present and no future. Nothing and no one existed for her now. She would simply disappear.

She heard the rumble of voices from the lounge as she tiptoed past the door. She thought she could hear Mr Martin's, but it must be her imagination. She slid out of the kitchen door, and dived hurriedly into a clump of rhododendrons. Three minutes later she was standing beside the main road waving her thumb for a lift. 'Bygone Antiques, Keswick.' The gold painted words flashed past her eyes as the very first vehicle slowed to a shuddering halt. She knew she was a fool to hitch on her own, but who cared, she had nothing to lose. As she ran towards the small green van and wrenched open the door, she thought she heard someone call her name from further up the road, so she leapt in and slammed the door without stopping to look at the driver. Would he be a rapist? Or would he simply kidnap her and ask a colossal ransom? Well, if he did he was out of luck, no one would pay a one penny piece to get her back. All the same it came as a delightful surprise to hear a woman's voice ask, 'Where to, kid?' Sheesha looked sideways through the gloom and saw a middle-aged woman, heavily made up and with hair of an unlikely shade of yellow. She held a cigarette between her fingers with their long red painted nails and for the next four hundred miles she was never without one for a minute. The word 'Keswick' floated into Sheesha's mind, and she said, 'I'm going to the Lake District for a few days before my exams.'

'You're in luck, kiddo,' commented the driver with a crackling smokers laugh. 'I'm headed for home, and that's right in the middle of the Lakes.'

'Thanks very much,' said Sheesha. 'Are you really an antique dealer?'

'Yep! Got me own shop in Keswick, but I've been down here on a buying trip. Got all sorts in the back, and when all the folks from Fleebridge come up on holiday, I'll sell it all back to them for double the price,' and she laughed again, enjoying her own joke enormously.

'I don't suppose your parents know you're hitching,' she commented, and Sheesha felt danger looming ahead.

'They think I'm going by train,' she lied with her well practised expertise. 'But this way I'll have more money to spend when I get there. I'll give them a ring when I arrive.'

'That's alright then, kiddo, but for one minute back there I thought you were running away. Now, you're going to have to work your passage. I've got to drive all night long, and I'll kill us both if I doze at the wheel, so you'll have to talk to me – that's why I picked you up. By the way – I'm Candy – Candy Forbes – now you fire away.'

Talking for eight hours non-stop was something Sheesha had never done before, but the story of her life was electrifying enough to keep a dormouse awake. Candy enjoyed the bits about the IRA man so much she had to pull on to the hard shoulder to get over a paroxysm of coughing induced by the excitement.

'That's what I like, kiddo,' she gasped. 'The spirit of adventure. It's the only thing that keeps life fun.'

She relished the bits about Zac, but Sheesha stopped short of the subject of Edward's death.

'If I had a man like your Zac,' Crackled Candy, 'I wouldn't take off without him, I can tell you.'

About five in the morning, both were wilting visibly, and Candy said, 'We're only a couple of hours short of home now. I'm going to pull into the next services, and we'll kip down for a while, then we can go in, have a wash and a coffee, and I'll be ready to open the shop at 9.30 am as usual.'

'You mean you're going to work all day without going

to bed,' said Sheesha horrified.

'You say you want to be a doctor, my girl, so you'd better get used to that kind of lifestyle too.'

Two hours later they were facing each other across the table in the motorway restaurant. Candy had spent half an hour in the ladies loo working on her face and hair, and she was now gulping black coffee as if it was heroin and she was an addict.

Sheesha had decided to make a large hole in her five pound note and had ordered bacon, sausages and chips.

'Ugh!' protested Candy shutting her eyes. 'The sight of that really punishes me at this time in the morning.'

Just as the last delicious forkful had disappeared Sheesha suddenly stiffened, covering her face with both hands.

'What's up now, kiddo?' demanded Candy.

'Have you got any dark glasses?' mumbled Sheesha through her fingers.

'Sunglasses, at seven o'clock on a foggy morning?' protested Candy. 'All that grease given you a migraine?'

'Quick, I'll explain in a minute, and lend us that scarf that's round your neck.'

Quite mystified but very intrigued, Candy obeyed. 'No one gets to have a quiet life with you around,' she commented as she watched Sheesha obscuring as much of her face as she possibly could.

'Those two men who just came in,' hissed Sheesha, 'don't look now, they're at the counter getting tea. One of them is my IRA man. I told you I'd know him again anywhere.'

'He's talking with an Irish accent alright,' said Candy doubtfully, 'but are you sure?'

'When a man's poked a gun at you twice and practically knocked your teeth out, you don't tend to forget easily,' said Sheesha dryly.

'Do you want me to go and ring the police?' asked Candy unenthusiastically.

172

'Oh no!' said Sheesha, that was about the last thing she wanted. 'They wouldn't be interested until we can tell them something definite.'

'Well I must say there are one or two things in the back of my van that I would rather unload before I meet the fuzz face to face,' admitted Candy. 'But what shall we do?'

'What should she do?' Sheesha wondered. There he sat, drinking his tea not two tables away. The man who had haunted her dreams and prevented her from walking across the common without frequent backward looks. The man the Chief Inspector had said might kill her if . . . They could sit here looking the other way and let them leave, then melt onto the motorway and escape. But this man was dangerous. He had hit her and burnt down the cottage she loved. A flash flood of anger gave her courage and anyway what did she have to lose?

'You did say the spirit of adventure makes life fun,' she said, 'so let's follow them.' When Candy smiled at her across the table, Sheesha couldn't help thinking she was one of the nicest people she had ever met.

'I'll just go and ring my partner,' said Candy. 'I'll say I got delayed on the trip, get her to open the shop and hold the fort until I get in. You stay there until I get back, and keep an eye on the little lambs.'

Twenty minutes later when a Datsun Stanza pulled out into the line of Northbound traffic, a small green van eased its way out behind it, just as the sun broke through the ceiling of fog.

It was about 9.15 am when they sailed past the signs for the Keswick turn-off.

'I wonder where they are heading,' said Candy.

'I have a terrible feeling I know,' said Sheesha as they flashed past a hoarding which said: SELLAFIELD NUCLEAR POWER STATION welcomes visitors.

'They wouldn't, would they?' whispered Candy in awe.

'If they put a bomb in there it would cause an international incident,' said Sheesha. 'Goodness knows what we can do to stop them.'

'I haven't felt so young in years,' giggled Candy, and pressed her foot further down on the accelerator.

'Sellafield visitor's centre welcomes the family', said another notice as they approached what looked like a science fiction studio set. 'They seem to be heading straight for the visitor's car park,' frowned Candy. 'They can't do much damage there, it's quite separate from the power station. They've got all kinds of exhibitions in there, working models, videos and computers, it attracts kids from all over the country. It's just a cover-up, really, to keep the public's mind off the dangers of fall-out, but it also takes their minds off buying antiques. They get hundreds through here every week.'

The Datsun pulled into the far corner of the car park which was practically deserted at that time of the morning. Candy parked facing them at a discreet distance, and lit yet another cigarette.

'What now then, kiddo?' she asked.

'We'll sit here and watch them,' replied Sheesha simply.

'Well, I'd feel happier if someone knew where we are, just in case things get nasty. No, its alright lovey, not the fuzz. I'm just going inside to phone my partner, I'll tell her everything, and she can ring Old Bill if we don't check in again this evening.'

'She's treating this like a huge game,' thought Sheesha, as she watched Candy hurry away. But she had to admit that it was working like a dose of morphine on the pain of her own deep injuries.

Before Candy got back from the phone, another car pulled into the car park and edged its way up beside the Datsun. Out climbed a burly man in a T-shirt and holiday trousers, and after a furtive look round he slid into the back seat of the Stanza.

'They got some company, then,' commented Candy as she slammed the door. 'I got more ciggies and some chocky for you.'

For two solid hours they sat puffing and nibbling and the sun began to beat on the roof of the van as the car park filled up around them with coaches, cars and hoards of sightseers. A mixture of heat, cigarette smoke and lack of sleep at last caused Sheesha to close her eyes. The silk scarf slipped off her head as it lolled against the side of the van and her sunglasses fell to the floor.

She was dreaming again. This time the Irishman was leaning in through the open window holding a gun at her nose.

'Don't move or make a sound or you've had it.' This voice was not inside her head, it was horribly real and she opened her eyes with a start. This was no dream, the only too familiar face behind the gun was leering at her yet again.

'The Holy Mother and all the saints keep sending you along to ruin every job I ever try,' he growled, 'but this one's too big for you to stop, young woman. Get into the back of the van, the both of you, and don't make a sound.'

'We can't do that,' protested Candy. 'We'd smash all my china.'

'Lady, if you don't, I'll smash more than your china!' threatened the man as he and his accomplice took the two front seats and Sheesha and Candy wriggled into the back. The car park was deserted, the sightseers were in the visitor's centre or sunbathing on the grass, so in no time they were both gagged and trussed up like Christmas trees in transit.

'Follow my car,' said the third man, above the ominous sound of smashing antique porcelain. 'We can dispose of these two and still be in time to do the job.'

'Nothing can hurt me now,' thought Sheesha wearily as she felt the van begin to move out of the car park, but she felt profoundly sorry for poor Candy.

Sheesha calculated that they could not have driven more than a mile or two at the most before they turned sharply to the right and proceeded to bump over a rough track.

'Make sure no one's about before you move them in,' hissed the man in holiday clothes. 'Don't forget I've been here for a week setting up this cover.'

'It's a fine day, they'll all be at the beach,' commented Sheesha's old friend, and soon they were being humped uncomfortably into what appeared to be a caravan. Sheesha had a fleeting impression of rows of other vans parked on a huge sweep of grass, and then she was being thrown down on a bed with enough force to wind her completely.

'Where do you come into all this?' one of the men demanded as he ripped the plaster from Candy's mouth.

'I'll tell you anything you like, if you'd only give me a cigarette,' she replied and received a smack on the face for an answer.

'Come on, be a gentleman,' she commented mildly.

'You went to make a phone call,' accused the man in the T-shirt. 'Was it to the police?'

'I rang my partner in my shop in Keswick,' replied Candy. 'I would never demean myself by ringing the fuzz.'

'You're lying,' said the Irishman hitting her again.

'Well, if you keep hitting me like this, I'll tell you any lie you like,' grumbled Candy, 'but that just happens to be the truth.'

'Leave the old cow alone,' said the other man. 'If she'd called the police they'd have been here by now. They've got nothing on us, our records are clean, that's why we were chosen for this job. Let's not waste time, we should do it now, today, before these two are missed.'

Someone regagged Candy and then all three men sat down round the folding caravan table.

'We should modify our plans, just go for the visitors centre restaurant – leave the other banger for a bit. If we go now, it'll be dinner time and we'll have the most clients.'

'You *sure* they never check bags?' demanded the man from Sheesha's nightmares.

'We went through that before,' was the angry reply. 'They only check if you are going on the bus tour round the power station but all you're going to do is have a cuppa in the cafe, then forget your beach bags when you leave. They are ready for you in the boot of my car. I only have to set the timer devices. On top's some swimming things, suntan cream and the remains of a picnic. If anyone glances in they won't look further than that.

'Now are you sure you know the procedure? You go into the cafe, order tea, and take a table right in the middle of the room. Slide your bags under the table, and then look as if you're going off to the loo. I've worked out exactly how long all that will take you, and I'll set the devices now. You'll only have about five minutes to get clear.'

'Only five minutes?' protested both men in unison.

'People won't bother about you for five minutes, they'll just think you're in the loo, after that someone's going to get suspicious about two abandoned bags. There'll be at least 100 people in there at this time of day, and the bangers will go off before anyone can do anything about it. You just walk slowly away, so no one notices you, and drive back here looking like holidaymakers.'

'What about these two cows?' inquired the first man.

'When you get back here we put a few pellets into them, lock the place up and drive out looking like we're off for a picnic. Easy as that!'

'Let me shoot'm now,' growled Sheesha's friend. 'I've been dreaming of this since last November.'

'Not yet. If anything goes wrong we may need them as hostages to get away. After all you have failed on your last two jobs.'

'But that was her fault both times,' he roared, 'that's why I want the pleasure of finishing her off myself.'

'Go on the pair of you,' ordered the boss, and he shooed them out of the caravan like a couple of stray hens, and then he sat down to watch them.

Chapter Sixteen

'I don't really mind dying,' prayed Sheesha, 'but please God, don't let all those holidaymakers and their kids die. I know I deserve to, but I'm sure they don't. And please take care of Candy.' Then she shut here eyes and thought of Zac. He was so far away – and she would never see him again now. He would always remember her as nothing but a murderer.

She had not lived happily ever after, as Manda had phophesied. No handsome prince would rescue this fairy-tale princess.

'It was really my fault I wasn't happy,' she thought. 'I never really gave Beth and Dad a chance. Underneath they were both hurting, yet all I ever thought of was how I felt myself. I could have done so much more to help them.' She remembered their stricken faces in the kitchen the last time she had seen them. 'If only I could do something to help them now,' she thought.

Suddenly a light tap on the door roused her, and the man with the gun sprang to his feet. 'Who's there?' he asked abruptly.

'It's just the boy from reception,' said a child's voice with an oddly familiar ring. 'I've got a telephone message for you.

Hastily the terrorist hid his gun in the locker and tweaked a curtain round the beds where Sheesha and Candy were lying.

Sheesha heard the door open, then a bang, a grunt and the sound of a heavy fall.

'The police,' she thought, not knowing quite if she was relieved or frightened. 'I'll pretend to be unconscious and shut my eyes.' She heard the curtains part abruptly and then someone with very strong arms was lifting her up and holding her very tightly, rocking her to and fro. She had never encountered a policeman like this before. Slowly she became conscious of a familiar exotic smell and she told herself she really must have gone out of her mind after all.

'I'm here, you're safe now,' murmered a voice in her ear, and at last she dared to open her eyes. With her hands tied tightly behind her and her mouth stuck over with plaster, there were not many ways of showing Zac how pleased she was to see him, but he was holding her so tightly, he must have heard her heart beating.

A moan from the man on the floor brought them both back to reality and Zac sprang into action. He soon had the ropes and gag off Sheesha and was using them to bind the IRA man who lay in a crumpled heap by the door.

Sheesha went to work on Candy, who said as soon as she could speak, 'Kiddo, if you'd told me he was this gorgeous, I'd have driven right back to Fleetbridge last night. How can you be so lucky?' Sheesha smiled at her fondly, and then suddenly she remembered all the holidaymakers who at that very moment were sitting in the cafe eating chips while death approached in two canvas beach bags.

'Zac, listen!' she said urgently. 'We've got no time to lose.' With amazing clarity that only a mind like hers could achieve she told Zac about the other two men and their deadly mission.

'I'll go and ring the police from the reception office,' he said diving towards the door, but Sheesha sprang up and caught him by the arm. 'Leave me out of this, I'll be gone by the time they get here,' she said.

'Stay until I get back,' he pleaded, and jumping onto a motor scooter he was soon bumping up the track between the caravans.

'You are running away from the fuzz, aren't you Kiddo?' said Candy when the sound of his engine had died away. 'Come on my girl, there's more to your story than you've told me so far.' And she sat down heavily on the chest of the man Zac had just tied up. 'I'm not taking any chances with this chap,' she remarked as she lit the inevitable cigarette.

'But *how* did you get here?' demanded Sheesha when Zac reappeared and had taken Candy's place on the prisoner's chest.

'I've been following you all night,' he smiled. 'I was coming to see you, when I saw you climb into a green van.'

'But what about Carolyn?' asked Sheesha blankly.

'Carolyn? Oh yes, that was earlier. I wanted to see you then, too, but she said you were all so devastated I'd be intruding. I've been kicking myself all night for listening to her. It took me a couple of hours to realize you might want a bit of reassurance and I was coming back when I saw you running awy. I noticed the name on the van and I thought if I could get myself to the shop in Keswick I could trace the driver and perhaps find out where you were heading. I thought about ringing the police, but I guessed you wouldn't like that, so I just hitched a lift myself. I had three really good rides and when I got to the shop this delightful lady told me just what had happened and where you were. She even lent me her motor scooter.'

'Well, I'll be jiggered,' snorted Candy. 'Queenie's usually so tight she wouldn't lend a bone to a starving dog.'

'Well, it's not my fault if I was born with charm,' smiled

Zac nonchalantly. 'Anyway, I got to the visitor's car park, where she said you were, just in time to see those rats pushing you into the back of the van. I do hope they didn't hurt you, Sheesha, I felt sick all over with worry about you.'

'Don't worry about her,' put in Candy. 'It's me they hit – good job I've got false teeth already.'

'I followed the car here on the scooter,' continued Zac, 'and hid behind the next-door caravan. I knew I couldn't take on all three men, and I was so worried I was just about to ring the police after all, when out came two of them and I got my chance.'

'I must go now,' said Sheesha, 'before the police come.'

'Don't,' said Zac, looking up at her with bleak misery in his eyes.

'But I can't just sit here and let them have me,' protested Sheesha.

'But if you disappear, I might never find you again,' said Zac, and all the usual self confidence had left his voice. 'Sometimes people run off and they're never seen again – they just vanish. I worried all night that I would never catch up with you again. I couldn't stand that.'

Candy blew her nose loudly, and became suddenly very absorbed in making up her face.

'But don't you realize what they'd do to me if . . . you've never been in a place like Parkfield, have you?'

'But you can't spend the rest of your life running away,' pleaded Zac, abandoning his post on the prisoner's chest and sitting down next to her on the bed. 'I know Edward's death wasn't your fault, I'll convince them all of it too, right up to the Prime Minister if necessary. Please trust me – and God.'

'You listen to him, Kiddo,' put in Candy through a cloud of smoke. 'You've probably saved a hundred lives – surely they'll all give you the benefit of the doubt.'

182

'Shall I trust him and God?' thought Sheesha. 'Or rely on myself like I always have?' Her decision seemed easy to make as she snuggled up closer to Zac and put her head down on his shoulder. Then she wondered what Manda would say if she could see her now.

Suddenly the ground under their wheels shook and a distant ominous rumble came to them through the summer breeze. They all leapt to their feet in horror, and the terrorist opened his eyes and smiled at them wickedly.

'Oh no!' gasped Sheesha. 'I prayed that wouldn't happen.' And Candy, disregarding her mascara, began to cry.

Zac kicked open the door of the caravan just as a car skidded to a halt on the dusty road outside. Doors banged and heavy feet ran towards them.

'You're useless! You weren't in time,' wailed Sheesha as three policemen burst through the door.

'Don't worry, lady,' smiled the one in plain clothes, 'we just heard on the car radio that the whole centre was cleared in time. No one's been hurt, and two men are in police custody – this man looks like number three, thanks to your quick thinking. The only damage done is to the Visitor's Centre, which seems to have been destroyed.'

'Well, that's the best thing the IRA ever did,' crackled Candy. 'Now all the tourists will leave those videos and come back to buying antiques.'

The rest of the day was a quite unbelievable whirl of activity. There were countless questions to answer, statements to make, prisoners to indentify, interviews with the press and TV cameras to face.

'Thank God I got my hair permed last week,' commented Candy happily. 'This is the biggest day of my life.'

It was nearly ten before they were allowed to leave

Whitehaven police station and Candy drove them back to Keswick in her van. 'We'll stop off at the chip shop,' she said, 'then you can both kip down in my pad.' Zac and Sheesha were so tired they could have slept in the street, but Candy was bursting with energy. 'Your generation's got no stamina,' she complained as she led the way up the stairs to her flat over the shop. 'I feel like a celebration,' she said. 'I could have paid out thousands on advertising and never got as much publicity as I have today!' And Sheesha and Zac groaned as they flopped down on the antique buttoned back sofa.

'You need coffee,' said Candy and it sounded like a threat, but at that minute the doorbell rang from somewhere down below them in the shadowy shop.

'I just couldn't look another reporter in the camera,' sighed Zac wearily.

'Come on!' protested Candy, 'it all helps my trade,' and she disappeared down the stairs.

It was the first time that Zac and Sheesha had been alone since the night that Edward had died, and they both started to say something at once.

'Go on. ladies first,' laughed Zac.

'I just wanted to say thanks for saving my life twice in one month,' smiled Sheesha shyly.

'There's an old Chinese proverb that says if you save a person's life twice they belong to you forever,' said Zac and he was not smiling now.

'I'm never going to belong to anyone but God,' said Sheesha, 'whatever the Chinese say, but I wouldn't mind being special friends.'

'Feminist,' he accused.

'Male chauvinist pig!' she countered.

'All the same, I think we'll get along very well,' said Zac, and standing up he pulled her into his arms.

'He's actually going to kiss me,' she thought weakly. But once again the beautiful bubble burst.

'Here they are,' said Candy's voice, 'and not wasting time either by the looks of it.' Sheesha gasped and shrank back into a shadowy corner as she saw who it was that followed Candy into the room.

'Beth,' she breathed, 'Dad.' Suddenly she was enclosed by masculine arms that were not Zac's and Beth was sobbing as she also hugged her stepdaughter.

'Can you ever forgive me?' she said. 'I didn't know what I was saying or doing that night.'

'As soon as we got the results of the postmortem this morning we ran up to your room, continued Michael, 'and we realized you had gone. It was our fault you had to suffer all this. We nearly went out of our minds all day until Zac rang.'

'We just couldn't bear to lose you,' put in Beth, 'the house is so empty without you.'

Was there really a place in this world for her after all? Was she actually loved and wanted in spite of all her failings and mistakes?

'But what about the police?' she faltered. 'I'll be arrested when I get back home.'

'They owe you an apology too,' said Michael gently. 'You see the postmortem showed that Edward was in the early stages of a respiratory infection, and he also had a quite undetected heart defect. The combination of the two were enough to cause his death, but the pathologist says it was quite obvious how hard you had tried to save him. Thank you for that, we shall never forget it.'

'Perhaps,' whispered Sheesha with a deep sigh as she looked up into the faces of Beth, Michael and Zac, 'perhaps now I really will live happily ever after.'

*New and recent titles in
Pickering Paperbacks*

THE BROKEN STONE   Jennifer Rees

An exciting-to-the-last-page novel triumphing in the power of Christ. Manda is troubled by her new foster-sister who insists on being called *Sheesha*, and who seems to have strange powers. Nevertheless she is drawn irresistibly to Sheesha's evil, which wreaks havoc and spreads terror both at home and at their school. Manda's fun-loving aunt, a Christian, and the local doctor, who is more than intrigued by Sheesha, show a way of escape which in absolute fear the girls turn to . . . with totally unexpected results.

*   *   *   *

CLAIRE'S CHOICE   Joan Selby-Lowndes

Claire, popular and pretty and content with everything around her, suddenly finds herself surrounded by trouble. She has sickening suspicions about her boyfriend Colin's trips out with the Neil gang, and her younger brother becomes sullen and aggressive as a result, Claire discovers, of sniffing glue. Her loyalties are turned inside out. Should she keep quiet and protect Colin? Should she hurt her parents by telling them about Graham, or would that be betraying her brother?

*   *   *   *

LIFELINE   Joan Selby-Lowndes

As the summer came near, all Tracey could dream of
was leaving school . . . no homework, a job, money
to spend as she pleased. Soaking up the first warm
sun with her friends, 'I want to be free,' she told
them. And then the worst news possible. She was
pregnant.

Having to make lifelong decisions was not part of
Tracey's plan at all. Yet through them she and all
her friends discover new truths about themselves
and about God.

If you wish to receive *regular information* about *new books*, please send your name and address to:

London Bible Warehouse
PO Box 123
Basingstoke
Hants RG23 7NL

Name _____

Address _____

_____

_____

_____

I am especially interested in:
- [ ] Biographies
- [ ] Fiction
- [ ] Christian living
- [ ] Issue related books
- [ ] Academic books
- [ ] Bible study aids
- [ ] Children's books
- [ ] Music
- [ ] Other subjects

P.S. If you have ideas for new Christian Books or other products, please write to us too!